"JESSE, DON'T!" SHE SCREAMED.

She let her bag slip to the floor as she sprinted down the corridor toward him.

He was hunkering on the sill before she'd covered half the distance to the window. With the same silly smile on his face, he turned back to her, gave a small wave of his hand, and stepped off the sill.

Dawn screamed as she saw him topple and fall. Then she threw herself the rest of the distance to the window.

There were several more screams from students still outside and then a squishy sort of crash. As Dawn stared down, she saw that Jesse had hit the path below and lay in a crumpled heap.

Dawn felt battered by sickness and shock. Her legs weren't able to support her any longer, and she slid to the floor.

She'd just seen Jesse Stern cheerfully step out of a third-floor window thinking he could fly.

Why?

Books by John Peel

TALONS
SHATTERED
POISON
MANIAC

Available from ARCHWAY Paperbacks

MANIAC

JOHN PEEL

AN ARCHWAY PAPERBACK
Published by POCKET BOOKS
New York London Toronto Sydney Tokyo Singapore

AN ARCHWAY PAPERBACK *Original*

An Archway Paperback published by
POCKET BOOKS, a division of Simon & Schuster Inc.
1230 Avenue of the Americas, New York, NY 10020

ISBN: 0-671-88735-1

First Archway Paperback printing June 1995

10 9 8 7 6 5 4 3 2 1

Cover art Gerber Studio

Printed in the U.S.A.

IL 7+

This is for our favorite teacher,
Arlene Moulder

MANIAC

Prologue: Friday Night

It was just a dream.

Jesse Stern was *almost* convinced of that. He lay on his back in bed, the top sheet crumpled and barely pulled up to cover his stomach. It had to be a dream he was having, even if he thought he was awake. Dreams were like that—very real sometimes.

He stared up at the shape above him. It was floating, mistlike, over his bed. It looked like a thin, wispy cloud, pale and slightly glowing, moving gently as though stirred by some air current Jesse couldn't feel. The gentle rippling effect on the whatever-it-was seemed almost soothing. He had to be dreaming this. What else could it be?

Jesse certainly didn't believe in ghosts, and this didn't appear to be any kind of haunting he'd ever heard about. The cloudlike shape hovering in the air was just too weird, but it didn't seem scary. He felt quite calm and relaxed. Even when the tendrils from the cloud slipped down gently to touch his bare arms, Jesse felt no alarm. The touch was the softness of a breeze. It seemed to stroke his arm, and then the cloud descended as if the whole of it were coming down to rest upon him.

Still, he was not disturbed. It was just a dream. Nothing more. Nothing to be bothered about.

Then pain shot through him, and his brain seemed to burn up inside his skull. He didn't have a chance to open his mouth and scream before his mind went blank, his body numb.

When he awoke in the morning, he shuddered as the memory flooded back to him. "That was the worst dream," he muttered to himself. Talk about a nightmare! He'd felt like he'd been dying. But it had been nothing, just a dumb dream. He stared at his bedside clock. Time to be up and out for another marvelous day of school. Not.

Reluctantly, Jesse swung his legs out of bed and stood up. He winced as a sharp pain stabbed through his right thigh. It hurt so badly, he almost fell down. Worried, he glanced down at his leg.

About three inches above his knee was a red welt. It felt as if the muscle underneath was on fire. Gingerly, he touched the red area. It was a bit sensitive, but that was all. After a moment he tried to put weight back on the right leg. There was only a twinge of pain, which quickly passed.

It was probably just some insect bite. Nothing to worry about. Nothing at all.

Heading for the bathroom, Jesse put the dream and the welt out of his mind. It was just one of those things.

That was the biggest mistake of his life. But it wasn't one he'd have to live with for long.

He had exactly forty-nine hours to live.

CHAPTER

1

"Hey, Carolyn! Candy! Wait up!"

Dawn Jacobs grabbed her bag and leaped out of her mother's car. She blew a quick kiss to her mother. "Thanks for the ride, Mom," she gasped before shooting off across the still-green, mid-September lawn toward Brookville High School.

"Think nothing of it," her mother called. "I spent all those years in med school just to drive you around."

Dawn hardly heard. She was struggling to pull her

pack onto her shoulder with one hand while waving to her friends with the other. Her mother had just finished a shift at Brookville Hospital and for once could actually drop Dawn at school. It didn't happen often, because Dr. Jacobs was the head of the emergency room at the hospital, and her hours were really strange, and overtime unfortunately was normal. Dawn didn't see as much of her mother as she'd like, so it was nice to get a chance to chat with her.

Carolyn and Candy stopped and waited for Dawn to catch up. Carolyn Rice had been Dawn's best friend since kindergarten. The two girls hadn't met Candace Watson until high school, but now the three of them really hit it off. Carolyn and Candy were both in the school orchestra—Carolyn loved her violin, and Candy was a pretty terrific oboe player. Other than that, the two girls couldn't have been less alike. Carolyn was slim—almost bony—with short-cropped dark hair and dreamy eyes that she insisted were the color of violets. Candy was a very lively and attractive blond who had boys swarming around her. Still, she didn't date much, spending most of her spare time practicing her music.

Dawn was a total loss at music. She had never even figured out a simple scale. Cats winced when she tried to sing. Actually, *she* hated her singing voice. It was good that her passion was for literature and not music. Dawn wanted more than anything to be a writer. Well, almost anything. She wouldn't have minded a few dates with Shane Morrow . . .

Dawn had inherited her mother's flame red hair and green eyes, along with a liberal sprinkling of freckles across her cheeks and shoulders. From her father she had picked up a chronic inability to arrive anywhere on time.

Puffing a little as she brushed stray wisps of hair out of her eyes, she greeted her friends. "So, what's new?"

"Not your top," Candy answered, grinning. "Didn't you wear that last Friday?"

Dawn glanced down at her green blouse. "Did I?" she asked blankly. "I don't remember."

"Honestly," Candy told her, "you *have* to pay more attention to your clothes. You want to be called a nerd?"

Dawn shrugged. "Hey, I've been called worse." This was, unfortunately, perfectly true. She thought she looked okay and couldn't understand some of her friends' obsession with clothes. She'd even worn the same outfit to school twice in one week, and probably would again.

"Lighten up, Candy," Carolyn added. "It's not like she's got a date or anything. It's only school."

"And how will she ever get a date if she doesn't pay more attention to what she wears?" argued Candy. "Guys like their dates in attractive wrappers, you know."

Dawn snorted. They entered the school together, heading for their lockers. "Guys like *you* in anything," she pointed out. "You could wear a garbage bag and they'd still be after you."

"Even with the garbage in it," added Carolyn.

"Ee-yew!" Candy stuck out her tongue. "Totally gross!" But she couldn't stifle a giggle.

The other kids were milling about in the usual antlike way, all trying to get where they were heading without paying attention to any other traffic. Someone barged into Dawn, almost sending her sprawling. Carolyn grabbed her arm, so Dawn managed to keep her balance.

"Hey!" Dawn yelled angrily as the guy who'd slammed into her walked on past. "What about an apology, jackass?"

The guy looked around, and Dawn recognized him—Jesse Stern. He was in her English lit class and generally a pretty okay sort of person. But today he looked—well, *weird.* His eyes were glazed over and vacant like there was no one home, his pale brown hair mussed. He jerked his head around, then continued wandering toward the stairs.

"Talk about rude!" snapped Dawn, her face red with anger. "What a jerk."

Candy frowned. "That's not like Jesse," she said. "He's usually very nice."

"And," added Carolyn, "he's usually drooling all down your front, Candy. He didn't even spare you a smile today."

Dawn was starting to calm down. Her back was a little sore where Jesse had elbowed her, but there hadn't been any real damage done. With her anger dulled, she realized that both of her friends were right.

Jesse hadn't just looked odd, he'd acted oddly, also. Plus . . . "Where's he going?" she asked. "He's got lit with me first period."

"His locker?" suggested Carolyn.

"It's on the ground floor," Candy pointed out. When Carolyn stared at her, wondering how she knew, she replied defensively, "All the cute guys in our classes have their lockers there. It's a fun place to hang out."

"So why is he going upstairs?" asked Dawn again.

"Who cares?" Carolyn said. "Maybe he's got bats in his belfry, and they're looking for somewhere new to roost." She shrugged. "If you're so concerned, why don't you follow him?"

"I'm *not* concerned," Dawn snapped. "It's just that he looked so weird. Like he was sick or something."

Carolyn smiled. "Your mom need new patients?" she asked. "And you're out recruiting?"

Dawn sighed. She wished she could just treat it like her friends were doing, but . . . Well, she couldn't get over that vacant expression on Jesse's face. It was like he wasn't really with them somehow. Knowing she'd probably regret it—she could hear Candy teasing her about being in love with Jesse already—she said, "I'll be back in a sec." Then she ran up the stairs.

Jesse was out of her sight until she reached the third floor. As Dawn stepped off the last flight of stairs, she spotted Jesse at the end of the corridor. His books were scattered along the floor, and he was unlatching the window there.

Dawn couldn't imagine what he was doing. "Jesse!" she yelled. "Wait up!"

He turned around and stared down the length of the corridor at her. "Hi," he murmured so she could barely hear him. "It's okay. I can fly."

"What?"

She jumped as the window catch suddenly sprung open and Jesse whipped the pane up. With a sudden rush of horror, Dawn realized he had to be totally out of his skull. "Jesse, don't!" she screamed. She let her bag slip to the floor as she sprinted down the corridor toward him. It was hard to believe they were the only two people in that short stretch of hallway, but the rooms right there were for storage and supplies. If only there was someone closer to him!

He was hunkering on the sill before she'd covered half the distance to the window. With the same silly smile on his face, he turned back to her, gave a small wave of his hand, and stepped off the sill.

Dawn screamed as she saw him topple and fall. Then she threw herself the rest of the distance to the window.

There were several more screams from students still outside and then a squishy sort of crash. As Dawn stared down, she saw that Jesse had hit the path below and lay in a crumpled heap, a red pool starting to seep out from under his body. People standing nearby had expressions of horror and shock on their faces—one girl collapsed.

Dawn felt battered by sickness and shock. Her legs weren't able to support her any longer, and she slid to the floor.

She'd just seen Jesse Stern cheerfully step out of a third-floor window thinking he could fly. She could only pray she hadn't seen him fall to his death.

CHAPTER

2

Hugging her knees, Dawn gripped her mug of hot chocolate and stared at her friends. Carolyn and Candy took the mugs that Mr. Jacobs had made for them. "I guess you want to talk," he said sympathetically. He closed the den door behind him as he went out.

Dawn, in her favorite chair, needed all the comfort she could get from her familiar surroundings. She was still in something like shock from the events earlier that day. She could remember the ambulance coming to pick up Jesse and her two friends staying with her while the school nurse checked her out. Then she was ordered home to rest. She just couldn't get the image of Jesse's cheerfully blank smile as he stepped off the windowsill out of her mind. Now that school was over, Candy and Carolyn had stopped by to check on her. Dawn's father had been home with her since he'd picked her up, fussing and clucking over her the whole time. She loved him dearly, but he'd overwhelmed her a bit with his caring. It felt better to be alone with her friends.

"Did you hear anything yet?" she asked them.

Carolyn shook her head. "Only that he was taken to emergency surgery. The principal promised a statement when he knew anything, but that was it."

"Wouldn't your mom know?" Candy asked.

"Yeah, I guess," Dawn agreed. "But she hasn't called or anything, and we never really know when she'll be home." She sipped at the chocolate. "I hope he's going to be okay."

"How do you feel?" Carolyn asked, reaching over to stroke the back of Dawn's hand.

"Mostly confused," Dawn admitted. "I mean, I *thought* there was something wrong with Jesse when he pushed me, but I never imagined it was so serious. I can't even begin to guess what was bothering him."

Candy shrugged. "Maybe he was on something?" she suggested. "Lots of kids are doing drugs."

"Not Jesse," Carolyn said firmly. "That's not his scene. He doesn't even drink coffee because of the caffeine."

"He's too straight for that kind of garbage," added Dawn.

"You never know what someone keeps hidden," Candy insisted darkly. "I mean, none of us knows him that well—unless one of you has been secretly dating him."

"I can't buy it," Dawn said. "It doesn't fit him." She shook her head. "Maybe it was a medical thing—stress or a chemical imbalance? Maybe he just flipped out."

Carolyn wrinkled her nose. "I doubt it. He's always been up there with straight A's and never sweated school or anything. He's one of those disgusting people who seems to thrive on exams. In fact, I'd say he was the closest thing to a genius we have in Brookville."

"They're the sort who snap," Candy said. "Maybe he was losing his grip and terrified of slipping down in the class rankings? There had to be a lot of pressure on him from his family and at school, even if it didn't show."

Dawn took another mouthful of the hot chocolate and swallowed. "What it all comes down to is that we don't have the slightest idea." The three of them finished their drinks in silence.

Carolyn sighed. "I've got to get going," she announced. "You feeling better now, Dawn?"

"Yeah." It was true; she was still confused and a little shocked, but her friends' visit had helped. "Thanks, guys."

"No sweat," Candy answered. "I'm going to run,

too. See you at school in the morning? Or are you going to try to con your folks into another day off?"

"I'll be there," Dawn promised. She saw her friends out. Neither lived too far away; the three families had all moved into the neighborhood when it had been built some fifteen years earlier. It was only because of weird school zone boundaries that Candy had attended a different elementary school.

Dawn's father popped out of his small library-cum-office. Dawn could see the glow of his computer screen in the background. "How are you feeling, sweetheart?" he asked.

"Better," she told him. "Thanks, Dad." She nodded at the office. "Work?"

"Yes." He made a mock grimace. "Sales figures for the quarter are due by the end of the week, and you know how my boss is."

She could see he was eager to return to his computer, but wasn't sure he should abandon her. "You'd better get back to those figures then," Dawn told him. "I'll be fine. I've got a new Diana Wynne Jones book to read, and I'm sure Mom'll be home soon."

Relief passed over his face. "Okay. But yell out if you want anything." He vanished back into his office.

Dawn smiled fondly after him, then collected the new book from her room. She'd been wanting to start it for a few days now. Diana Wynne Jones had always been one of her favorite authors in her favorite field—fantasy. Her tales were wildly inventive, and with a strong dose of humor. Dawn loved such stories; in fact, she was in the process of writing one of her own. She hadn't told Carolyn or Candy about it because she wasn't sure how good the story was. Maybe when she'd written more of it, she'd have one of them read it. Till then, it was going to remain her secret. Meanwhile, she could settle down, do a little reading, and see how a professional writer put it all together.

This time, though, she simply couldn't concentrate. It wasn't the fault of the book; she simply couldn't erase the picture of Jesse jumping from her mind. He was haunting her thoughts. Eventually, she put the book down without even marking her place. She couldn't recall anything she'd read, anyway, so she'd have to start it again when she was less preoccupied. She decided to make some coffee and wandered into the kitchen to do so. It would be nice to surprise her father with a cup; he swam in the stuff while he was working.

As she busied herself with the cups and the water, she kept seeing Jesse's face and hearing his words: "It's okay. I can fly." How could he have been so crazy as to believe that? He *had* to know that nobody can fly—at least, not outside an airplane or one of her science-fiction novels.

She supposed that Jesse must have been suffering from some sort of delusion because he had sounded completely sincere. He hadn't been trying to kill himself. He had, for whatever weird reason, really expected to step out of that window and fly. It was the kind of thing she'd heard three-year-olds do after watching *Superman* on TV, but not the kind of thing any level-headed seventeen-year-old would do in his wildest dreams.

Except . . .

Wildest dreams . . .

Dawn smiled ruefully as she filled the two cups. She could remember those dreams she'd had in which she could fly. It was a common sort of dream, she knew—to float gently over the landscape. Next to the one about wandering around naked and being laughed at, she supposed it was the most common dream in the world. But it was one thing to *dream* about being able to fly and quite another to actually believe you could do it.

Her father was grateful for the coffee, and Dawn then went into the living room with her own. She was still lost in thought when she heard a car pull into the garage. That had to be Mom coming home at last! Dawn called out, "Mom's home!" to her father, then dashed into the kitchen to put some water on to boil. Her mother was probably dying for a hot drink.

A moment later Dr. Jacobs came in from the garage. She was tired and pale and looked a lot older than she was. There were dark rings under her eyes that weren't from smeared mascara. She ran a hand through her disheveled hair, then tossed her coat over the back of a kitchen chair. That wasn't like Mom; she was normally a fanatic for tidiness.

"Hi, Mom," Dawn greeted her. "Rough day?"

"The pits," her mother answered. "How are you feeling?"

"Not as bad as you, by the looks of things," Dawn

answered. "What happened?" Then a sudden stab of fear spread out from her stomach. "What about Jesse?"

Dr. Jacobs put an arm around her daughter's shoulder. "He's dead, I'm afraid."

"Oh, God." Dawn collapsed into one of the chairs, feeling faint. "I can't believe it," she muttered.

"Me neither," her mother said. She shook her head. "Did you know him well?"

"So-so," admitted Dawn. "We had a few classes together, and he was kind of okay. He had the hots for Candy."

"Most boys do, I gather." Mom tried to crack a smile, but it wouldn't come. "He wasn't into anything —*drugs?"*

Dawn stared at her mother, puzzled. "I don't think so." She frowned, trying to concentrate. "I didn't realize how hurt he was, but the fall must have done a lot of damage, I guess."

"Oh, that's for sure," her mother agreed. "But it wasn't the fall that killed him." She sighed. "It's days like this I wish I wasn't a doctor."

Dawn's father had appeared just then; he must have finished his work on the computer. "Because you hate losing patients?" he said with sympathy.

"Because I wish I could get drunk without knowing the damage I was doing to my system."

"That bad?" asked Dad. He gave his wife a hug. "It's not easy to see a kid die, is it?"

"It's even worse when you can't even explain *why* he died," she replied.

"What do you mean?" asked Dawn. It was bad enough that someone she knew had died, but her mother's answers were starting to scare her. "You did say the fall hadn't killed him."

"But I can't tell you what did," Mom admitted. "We did everything we could to save him. He *should* have lived. He'd have been in pain and maybe crippled, but he should have lived. But—" She shook her head tiredly. "There was nothing there. *Nothing.*"

"You mean," Dad asked gently, "that he didn't want to live? That he'd tried to kill himself?"

"No!" her mother said vehemently. "I mean that there was nothing there. When he was wheeled into the ER, we hooked him into the EEG—electroencephalograph, which reads brain waves—and it was almost blank."

Dad frowned. "You mean he was brain damaged?"

"No. I mean it was as if his brain had been switched off. I've never seen anything like it, and I've seen plenty of weird things. There weren't even delta waves."

"I'm an ignorant businessman," Dad chided. "What does that mean?"

Mom did manage a smile at that. "Delta waves are common when a person is unconscious or drugged or has severe brain damage. But there were no signs of them."

Dawn was shocked at the tone in her mother's voice. It was clear that she was at a loss to explain Jesse's death. "You mean," she asked slowly as a creeping coldness clawed its way up her spine, "that he just died for no reason. Just like he walked out of a window for no reason?"

Mom answered gently, "He must have had *some* reason for both of them. It's just that none of us can figure out what it was." She sighed. "I know the police were almost hoping he was on drugs, but I didn't see any sign of them. Of course, they'll do a full blood work-up, and maybe something will turn up in the autopsy. But at the moment, nobody has an answer for anything that happened today."

Dawn shivered. What had happened to Jesse? What made him think he could fly—and then killed him without leaving a trace?

CHAPTER 3

The next three days were thankfully quiet except for the very sad occasion of Jesse's funeral. Dawn tried to settle back to the routine of school, but it was almost impossible to get the images of Jesse out of her mind. A cloud seemed to be cast over the school, and a permanent chill in the air. Even Candy was more subdued than normal, and nothing much ever affected her. Her flirting with boys had almost come to a halt, but the boys didn't seem to be missing it.

Part of the problem was the loss of Jesse, of course.

The other was that after three days of searching, neither the doctors nor the police had any idea about the reasons for his death. Dawn's mother had read all the autopsy notes and the police report, struggling to see if there had been something she had missed, something she might have done to save the boy's life, but there was nothing.

"He was in perfect health," she had growled over her morning coffee. "No heart trouble, no weird chemicals—nothing." She shook her head. "The worst thing he had was a small lump on his thigh, maybe a tiny cyst. But nothing that could have made him freak out, let alone kill him."

Before school on Friday Dawn told Carolyn and Candy the news. "It's just so bizarre," she said. "I wish there were some answers. I think they'd make me feel better."

"You, me, and the rest of the school," Carolyn muttered. "Everybody is really spooked. Even Candy."

Candy glared at her friend. "I am *not* spooked," she snapped.

"Yeah?" Carolyn raised an eyebrow. "Then how come you're wearing the same top you wore on Monday?"

Candy looked down and then frowned. "Did I wear this on Monday? I don't remember."

Dawn managed a smile. "That's *my* line," she said.

Tossing her golden curls, Candy sniffed. "Well, I *like* this top." Then she smiled. "I guess I just forgot. We've all had a lot on our minds since Monday."

"Yeah." Dawn led the way inside the building. "Well, I'll see you guys next period, I guess." She had English lit first, while her friends had music. With a wave, she headed for Mr. Belding's class.

This was her favorite subject—partly because she really loved books and partly because she wanted to be a writer, but mostly because Mr. Belding was a terrific teacher. He managed to breathe life into the stories they studied, and he conveyed his passion for the material to the whole class. It didn't hurt that he was also good-looking and fascinating. More than one girl in the class had dreams about him. Dawn hadn't that bad a crush on him, but she did like him an awful lot. It had broken several hearts when he and the music teacher, Miss Burton, had gotten married in June. They had honeymooned most of the summer in some small village in France. Dawn thought it was terribly romantic.

Reaching the classroom, Dawn saw that she was almost late. There were only a couple of seats left. One was by Martin Brewer, whom she couldn't stand. Another was by Andrea Calloway, who was a pain. The last one was directly behind Shane Morrow and his friend Vince Holloway. After a second's thought Dawn slid into that seat. Shane glanced around and gave her a half smile, then returned to his low-level discussion with Vince.

Dawn wished she could think of some excuse to chat with Shane. She couldn't help hoping he'd pay more attention to her. He was a really nice guy, not too tall, with sandy blond hair and a nice, friendly smile. Not a hunk exactly, but close to it. Vince, on the other hand, was a bit of a nerd. He was thin and gawky and constantly apologized for knocking things over. The problem was that he was always thinking about one thing while his body was doing another. Still, he meant well, and he was the only other person in her class who really liked science fiction. Shane was more into horror stories and real-life weird events, like UFOs and stuff.

She wondered what he thought about what had happened to Jesse. He had a whole shelf of books at home, he'd once mentioned, that dealt with all kinds of strange events. Maybe there was something in one of them that could explain Jesse's odd behavior? *That* was a point to start a conversation on, and she was about to try it when Mr. Belding walked in and class began.

Mr. Belding reminded them that it was time to start working on a writing assignment for the class, and Dawn realized that she hadn't decided what to do. The past few days she'd been too preoccupied with Jesse to consider a topic. When class was over, she started to rush out to meet Carolyn and Candy, but Mr. Belding called to her. She went back to his desk where he was putting his notes away.

"Have you thought about your writing project yet?" he asked her.

Dawn flushed guiltily. It was as if he'd been reading her mind! "Uh, well, I haven't decided on anything yet," she admitted.

Mr. Belding smiled. "That's what I guessed," he said. "Well, if you want a suggestion, I ran across something while I was in France that I thought would appeal to you or Vince."

Curious, Dawn asked, "What is that?"

"Well, we were staying in a small, out-of-the-way village in the French Pyrenees called Balbec. Miss Burt"—he grinned—"*Mrs.* Belding was studying musical styles. Anyway, I did a bit of research into local history and discovered a strange legend about the town." He pulled a thin book from his briefcase. "Apparently, during the Middle Ages, Balbec was supposed to be a doorway into Fairyland. A lot of odd things happened there, and several villagers claimed that Oberon, king of the fairies, appeared there at night. When I heard that, I immediately thought about you. I know how you love fantasy and science fiction, and I managed to find a book in English that covered the legend." He handed it to her. "So why not use it as the basis for your project? Maybe do something about the role of fairies in the literature of the Middle Ages or something? Combine business with pleasure?"

Dawn took the book with interest. She felt really pleased that he'd thought about her, even when he had much more interesting things to do! "Thank you," she said. "I'll take good care of it, I promise. And it sounds like a great idea."

"I thought it might appeal to you." He smiled. "And I'm looking forward to whatever you come up with, Dawn. You're always a delight to read. Maybe one day you'll turn out a book or three of your own."

Dawn blushed again. "I wish," she said. "I'd really like to."

"Then *do* it," he told her. "If you want something badly enough, you can always make it happen." He grinned again.

Dawn nodded and excused herself. She had to join Candy and Carolyn for gym. She slipped the book into her bag, then headed off to the gym. By the time she reached the locker room, her friends were already half changed.

"Trying to cut gym?" Carolyn asked.

"Mr. Belding wanted to talk to me," Dawn explained, slipping off her top and starting to change as quickly as she could.

"He's married," Carolyn shot back. "And I thought you had your eye on Shane, anyhow?"

"About my class project," Dawn said. "Honestly, get your mind out of the gutter."

"Why?" asked Carolyn, grinning. "It's more interesting watching life from down there. Isn't it, Candy?"

"Mmm?" Candy blinked and then looked at them. "I'm sorry. What?"

"Earth to Candy," Carolyn said, waving her hand in front of Candy's face. Candy batted it away. "What's with you today?" Carolyn asked. "You're really out of it."

"Just preoccupied, I guess," Candy admitted.

Dawn finished changing. "Okay, let's go, guys." The

three of them headed for the gym. They arrived just in time to be put into one of the practice teams for basketball. It wasn't one of Dawn's favorite games, but she was okay at it. On the other hand, it was good she never planned to go to college on a sports scholarship. She missed as many shots as she sank. Carolyn was a little better, and so was Candy—usually. Better coordination, Dawn guessed. But how coordinated did you have to be to work a word processor to write a novel?

It became increasingly obvious that something was bothering Candy. She began by missing passes by miles, and her shooting was even worse. Dawn had never seen her friend like this. During a rest, she grabbed Candy's arm.

"Are you okay?" she asked. "You're really screwing up today."

"I just can't focus," Candy admitted. "I don't feel so hot."

Carolyn placed her palm on Candy's forehead. "You feel okay to me," she said. "But what do I know about fevers or medicine? Maybe you should ask to be excused and go see the nurse?"

After a second's pause Candy nodded. "Yeah. I guess I should."

"You want me to come with you?" offered Dawn. "I don't think the team will miss me, the way I'm playing."

"No, it's okay," Candy answered. "I promise not to faint or anything."

"Any excuse to skip gym," said Carolyn to Dawn. "Nice try, though."

Candy went over to the coach, then left the gym. Dawn glanced at the clock. Only ten minutes to go. They could check on Candy at the nurse's between classes. It was probably nothing serious. Maybe it was just a touch of depression. Candy had always claimed that Jesse Stern was a pest, but Dawn guessed she was missing him pretty badly.

The rest of the period went quickly, and then the coach dismissed them for showers. Dawn ran to the locker room to get out of her sweaty clothes. Then she paused, puzzled. "Weird."

"What is?" Carolyn followed her gaze.

Candy's locker was open, and her clothes were still hanging in it.

"Maybe she's in the shower?" suggested Dawn. "She wasn't moving too fast."

"I don't think so," said Carolyn. "Here's her towel on the floor, and it's damp. She must have come out. So why didn't she get dressed?"

Dawn looked around and saw a small bundle on the floor. "Those are her gym clothes," she said slowly. It wasn't making any sense. What had happened to Candy? Where was she?

The door to the locker room opened, and Andrea Calloway poked her head in. She was grinning like a maniac and giggled when she saw Dawn and Carolyn. "You guys have *got* to see this!"

"Not now, Andy," said Dawn. "We're worried about Candy. Have you seen her?"

Andrea's grin got even wider. "Oh, yeah—lots of her. And so has half the school. Come on!"

Puzzled and worried, Dawn sprinted for the door with Carolyn just behind her. When they dashed into the corridor, Andrea pointed down the hallway. Dawn stared in shock and disbelief and immediately understood the reason for Andrea's dumb joke.

A crowd of students had gathered in the hallway. The boys were staring, some red faced. Most of the girls acted shocked; a few were giggling. Walking slowly, dreamily, down the corridor in front of them was Candy.

Stark naked.

Dawn and Carolyn stared at each other, stunned. What on earth did Candy think she was doing? Carolyn managed to speak first. "I know I told her she looked good in *anything,* but I meant *something,* not *nothing!"*

"Talk about showing off," Andrea gasped between giggles. "She's *never* going to live this one down!"

Finally managing to get her act together, Dawn ran down to where Candy was slowly wandering with a sappy smile on her face. She seemed totally unconcerned that she wasn't wearing anything. Looking around, Dawn found herself staring into Shane Morrow's face.

"Getting a good look?" she snapped, annoyed.

Shane blushed, then hastily whipped off his sweatshirt and held it out. There was a chorus of groans from most of the other guys. Dawn snatched the shirt from Shane and turned back to Candy.

"Candy," she said firmly. "Come on, put this on."

Her friend stared vacantly at her. "It's okay, Dawn," she said sleepily. "I'm only dreaming."

"She's dreaming?" one of the guys yelled out. "Me, I'm for lettin' her dream on!"

Dawn was furious at them. "She's *sick!"* she yelled out.

"And I'm lovesick," someone called.

Dawn shook her friend. "Candy, snap out of it! Don't you realize what you're doing?"

Candy just continued to smile. "I'm dreaming," she murmured.

"Then dream you're putting this on," growled Dawn, holding out the sweatshirt. Candy didn't react.

Shane stepped forward. "Candy," he said gently. "Raise your arms." He was obviously fighting an urge to look down. Candy obediently raised her arms. Dawn hastily tugged the shirt over her head and arms. There was a chorus of booing as she finally managed to get Candy covered. Shane then gently took one of Candy's arms and lowered it. He glanced at Dawn, acting a little ashamed. "Uh, maybe we'd better get her to the nurse?" he suggested.

"Definitely." Dawn stared at the crowd of students, which was starting to disperse now that there was nothing more to see. She wished she had a machine gun but knew she really couldn't blame them for their reactions. They were just being dumb.

But what was wrong with Candy? Why was she behaving so strangely? And why did she seem to think she was dreaming?

CHAPTER

4

Less than half an hour later Candy had been rushed off to the hospital. The nurse had been unable to explain Candy's odd condition or to snap her out of it. Carolyn had brought Candy's clothes from the locker room, so she'd been decent when she left. Dawn was able to give Shane his sweatshirt back.

"Thanks," she told him, still a little annoyed with him for having stared at her friend.

"Glad I could help," he mumbled. As he pulled the shirt back on, he said, "I should have done it earlier, shouldn't I?"

Dawn glared at him. "And miss the sights?" she snapped.

He flushed. "Well, I was kind of—distracted from thinking straight."

"It's not your fault," she said, trying to sound reasonable. "I can't blame you for staring at the prettiest girl in school."

"She's not," Shane said quickly. Then he blushed again. "Look, I hope she's okay," he added, then dashed off.

Dawn wasn't sure what to make of the conversation, but she was too worried about Candy to think about it now. Carolyn punched her gently on the arm.

"He's got the hots for you," she announced.

"What?" Dawn dragged her thoughts back. "Are you kidding?"

"Nope. Trust me on this one. I know the signs. He only has eyes for you."

"It was *Candy* he was staring at," Dawn replied.

"Well, you can't blame him for checking her out," Carolyn answered. "And he *was* the only one who offered his shirt to help you."

Dawn dismissed the idea. "What do you think is wrong with her?" she asked, the concern in her voice obvious.

"A bad case of exhibitionism?" suggested Carolyn. "I mean, I know Candy loves attention, but this is going too far even for her. She's going to get suspended for this one, if she's not expelled."

"I don't think Candy knew what she was doing,"

objected Dawn. "She told me that it was okay because she was dreaming."

"Is she ever going to get a rude awakening then." Carolyn grimaced. "I don't think anyone is going to buy that excuse."

Dawn sighed. "Carolyn, I don't think it was an excuse. Come on, Candy's a show-off, but *stripping* in front of the whole school? She's not that . . ." Her voice trailed off as a sudden thought occurred to her. "Wait a minute—you knew Jesse Stern better than I did. What was it he was always telling everyone he wanted to do after he graduated?"

"Are you kidding?" Carolyn snorted. "Ever since grade school, he had only one goal in mind: He wanted to be a pilot. I think he'd even signed up for the Air Force."

Dawn nodded. "That's what I thought. And the last thing he said to me was 'It's okay; I can fly.'"

"Not without a plane he couldn't," Carolyn said grimly.

Dawn was sure she was on to something now. "But it was what he wanted more than anything. It was what he dreamed of. He wanted to fly, and he thought he could. And now there's Candy . . ."

Carolyn stared at her, then shook her head. "You're saying that Candy wants to be a stripper when she grows up?"

"No." Dawn was still trying to work it out. "But she *does* love attention, and she certainly got it. And maybe she wouldn't do the nudist routine except in her wildest dreams—but I think that's where she *thought* she was—in a wild dream. She didn't know she was awake. Haven't you ever had a dream in which you were naked and didn't really care?"

Carolyn managed a smile. "You kidding? I have them all the time. But I know they're just dreams. Like the ones in which I play the violin so fast I saw it in half. They're just dreams."

"Right," agreed Dawn. "But I think Candy somehow couldn't tell she wasn't dreaming. Just like Jesse couldn't tell *he* wasn't dreaming. And they were both doing what they most wanted to do—Jesse was flying, and Candy was getting attention."

Carolyn stared at her. "I think *you're* the one who needs waking up, kid," she said. "Okay, they may have been living out dreams, but *why?* I mean, Candy was acting a bit odd today, but she didn't look like she was having a breakdown. So why would she start thinking she was dreaming when she was wide awake?"

"I don't know," admitted Dawn. "But it *can't* just be a coincidence that both she and Jesse acted so bizarrely in the same week. There's got to be a connection somewhere. Therc's *got* to be." But she still couldn't see what it might be.

After school Dawn was surprised to see her father waiting in the parking lot for her. She and Carolyn hurried over. "What's wrong?" she asked, worried.

"Nothing much," he replied. "I finished my reports, and my boss loved them so much he gave me the rest of the afternoon off. I called your mother, and she told me that Candy had been admitted to the hospital, so I figured you guys might want to stop by. And maybe grab a bite to eat out."

Dawn smiled happily. "Terrific. Thanks, Dad."

"Way to go," agreed Carolyn as they clambered in the car. "I just have to call my folks and let them know when we get to the hospital."

"Good idea," he agreed.

Happy that they'd get to see their friend, Dawn wondered if anything had been discovered yet. Mom would know. Hopefully, Candy would be better in a day or so. When they reached the hospital, her father led them in to admissions, where he asked about Candy's room.

"She's not allowed to receive visitors right now," the clerk replied. "She's still under observation."

"Bummer," muttered Carolyn. Dawn's heart sank.

"Then could you buzz Dr. Jacobs for me?" Dad asked. "Tell her that her husband and daughter are here." As the receptionist did so, he winked at Dawn. "Maybe Mom will let you know what's happening. I know you must be worried."

That was an understatement. Dawn was getting extremely concerned. Candy must have been there for about four hours, and they were *still* running tests on her? Hadn't they figured it out yet?

A few minutes later her mother came out of one of the corridors and hurried across to them. She looked tired and worried and ushered the three of them away from the steady stream of visitors and staff passing through the hospital entrance. "I've only got a couple of minutes," she said. "It's been a rough day."

"What about Candy?" Dawn asked anxiously. "Is she going to be okay?"

"Do you know what's wrong with her yet?" added Carolyn, just as worried.

"I'm not totally up to date," Mom admitted. "She's not in emergency, because she's not in a life-threatening situation. Dr. Calfa's in charge, but I did ask him to keep me updated. I knew you'd be concerned. Anyway, the last I heard she's in some sort of shock. It's really weird, but she seems to be dreaming while she's awake."

"Like Jesse Stern," said Dawn.

"Not exactly," her mother answered. "That was the first thing that occurred to me, too. It would be too much to accept as coincidence that both of them fell ill so close together, so I suggested an EEG. I figured that Candy's patterns might match Jesse's—the weird skewing of the brain waves. But they were almost exactly the opposite. Her alpha and beta waves—the ones that should be strongest while you're awake and alert—were really low, and her theta waves—thc ones that indicate dreaming, unconsciousness, or brain damage—are peaking like crazy."

Dawn felt faint. "You mean she's got brain damage?" she gasped.

"Not that we can tell," her mother answered. "To be honest, Dr. Calfa is baffled. He's ordered a battery of tests, and they're still running them. That's why she's not allowed visitors. They're hoping to find some sort of infection or drug that's causing her condition. I'll know more when I finish tonight. But right now, to be truthful, we're completely in the dark. The closest I can say is that Candy seems to be utterly lost in a dreamlike state, and we don't know if we can wake her."

CHAPTER 5

Dawn's entire weekend was completely taken up with worrying about Candy. When Dr. Jacobs had returned home that Friday evening, she had nothing positive to tell her daughter. There was no sign of drugs in Candy's system—Dawn had never expected there would be—no sign of any infection in her blood, no sign of brain damage or concussion. In fact, the tests showed there was absolutely nothing wrong with Candy.

Except that she was dreaming constantly and still awake.

Over the next two days, Dawn became more and more worried. So many tests had been run on Candy that she worried her friend probably wouldn't have any blood left. The doctors had run everything they could think of, and still they hadn't a clue as to what was happening.

And Candy was still dreaming while wide awake. That was the scariest thing.

Dr. Jacobs had explained the problem to Dawn. "Dreaming is only *part* of what happens when you sleep. Most people dream only a little each night, and the remainder of the time their brains rest. Candy's mind *isn't* resting. It's going constantly, and that can't be good for her. And it's also during rest that the body repairs itself. There's less demand for action on the heart and so forth, so that's why you feel refreshed after a good night's sleep. But Candy isn't getting any sleep at all. Her body's bound to get weaker if she doesn't fall asleep soon."

Dawn chewed at her lower lip for a moment. "Can't they give her something to make her sleep?" she finally asked.

"Yes, of course they could. Dr. Calfa may have to do just that. But no one wants to use drugs on her unless they can be sure it won't have a really serious side effect. But after a couple days without sleep, and with all of that mental activity, they're frankly running out of alternatives." She shook her head, exasperated and tired. "None of us has ever seen anything like this."

"Except in the case of Jesse Stern," said Dawn.

Her mother shrugged. "Maybe. It's possible that he

went through what Candy's going through, and that his weird EEG readings were a result of his mind undergoing complete collapse. But we just don't *know."* She sighed. "And there doesn't seem to be any connection between the two of them apart from the obvious one that they both go to Brookville High." She shook her head. "They weren't dating, didn't see each other very often, and took very few classes together. They lived on opposite sides of town and didn't even hang out at the mall together."

Dawn could sympathize with her mother. It seemed as if there was nothing to link the two sick kids at all—except there obviously *had* to be a link.

The whole weekend was a real drag. Even when Dawn's father took her and Carolyn to the mall, Dawn couldn't work up any enthusiasm. It seemed wrong to be out enjoying herself when her second-best friend was in the hospital.

The only up part of the weekend was an unexpected call on Sunday evening from Shane Morrow. Puzzled, Dawn took the call when her father told her who it was. "Hi, Shane. What's up?"

He sounded embarrassed and nervous. He'd *never* called her before and hardly spoke to her at school. She wondered why he was calling now. "Um," he said. "I was wondering if you'd heard anything about Candy?"

Dawn felt a pang of jealousy. *That* was why he'd called! He wanted an inside source for information about Candy. "Not much," she said, refusing to let her anger take over. "She's still sick, and the doctors don't know why."

"That's terrible," Shane replied. "I know she's your friend, and you must be really worried about her. Uh, if there's anything I can do to help, just let me know."

"Nobody but the doctors can help right now," Dawn said tightly.

"I didn't mean *her,*" Shane blurted out. "I meant *you.* Sorry, guess I was way out of line."

Dawn realized that she'd misjudged Shane. He'd called because he wanted to help, not to get information. "I'm sorry, Shane," she said meekly. "Of course you're not out of line. I really appreciate the offer." She felt warm and pleased at his attention. "I'll let you know. See you at school tomorrow, okay?"

"'Kay," he agreed happily and hung up.

Dawn replaced the receiver with a smile on her face. Finally Shane was paying attention to her! Maybe . . . Then the memory of Candy resurfaced, and her joy faded with it. It wasn't right to be thinking of dating when Candy was so sick.

Her father threw her a knowing look. "Boyfriend?" he asked.

"No," she said firmly.

He smiled. "Must be serious, in that case." He went back to reading his newspaper. Dawn would have felt better if the headline hadn't been MYSTERIOUS DISEASE AT LOCAL SCHOOL over a photo of Candy.

Dawn picked up her Diana Wynne Jones novel again and tried reading. But once more she couldn't concentrate. Normally, she'd be devouring this latest tale of magic, mystery, and strange jokes. Now, though, her mind was preoccupied with Candy and Jesse.

What could have made them both play out their innermost thoughts?

And—would there be others?

The next day was a little better because school distracted Dawn from her gloomy thoughts. Carolyn wasn't quite as moody as Dawn because she'd practiced her violin all weekend, and that was intensive concentration.

Dawn hurried along to her English lit class and found Shane there already. He was eagerly looking at the door as she went through it. He blushed and gave her a shy smile. The desk behind him was empty again, and he glanced back at it. Dawn nodded and sat there. "Hi."

"Hi," he greeted her. "Any more news?"

"No," she said, sighing.

"About what?" asked Vince, who was sitting next to Shane. He was skimming through a book with a very blurry photo of a UFO on the cover.

"About Candy Watson," said Shane with more patience than Dawn could have gathered together. He was obviously used to Vince being out of this world.

"Oh, yeah," Vince said, returning to his book. "Sad."

Shane fidgeted in his chair. "Uh, you doing anything after school?" he asked Dawn.

Dawn raised an eyebrow. This was definitely interesting. What a day to pick, though! "Yeah," she said.

His face fell. "I promised Carolyn I'd wait for her. She has orchestra practice."

"Oh" was all Shane said.

"It could be kinda dull," Dawn added. "You could maybe wait with me?"

That produced a smile. "Yeah, I'd like that."

"Like what?" asked Vince, realizing that the conversation wasn't over yet.

"Watching orchestra practice," Shane told him.

"Okay," said Vince. "But it sounds weird to me."

Before Dawn could explain that the invitation had been for Shane, not both of them, Mr. Belding arrived. As soon as she saw him, Dawn remembered the book he'd lent her—it was still sitting in her locker. After the events of Friday, she'd completely forgotten about her book project. She winced. Well, she'd take the book home with her that night and skim through it to see if it gave her any ideas. Right now, though, she had to concentrate on Dickens.

And think about how Shane was finally showing an interest in her.

Orchestra practice was well underway when Dawn slipped into the back of the auditorium. Shane was already there, waiting with an eager expression on his face. Unfortunately—Dawn couldn't help wincing—Vince was there also, but a few seats away from Shane, his face buried in the book he'd been reading earlier.

Well, maybe he'd stay out of this world while she and Shane chatted.

She wasn't entirely certain what Ms. Burton—oops! *Mrs.* Belding!—was having them practice. Dawn liked music, but the classics weren't her favorites. She could tolerate them, though, and identify a few. This was most likely a piece by Vivaldi that she couldn't place. After his famous *The Four Seasons,* Dawn was lost. Carolyn, on the other hand, had about thirty CDs of his music and adored the ones performed by the young Canadian cellist, Ofra Harnoy. Dawn preferred Garth Brooks any day.

She gave Shane a smile. "Hi."

"Hi." He shifted to make room. Dawn sat down and left a seat vacant between them, preferring a little space. The silence between them was filled only by the sounds of the orchestra and Vince turning a page rather noisily.

Dawn knew she had to say something. She had Mr. Belding's book with her, so she asked, "Have you decided what you're doing for the lit project?"

Shane grimaced. "I'm still working on it. I was thinking of doing something about Robert Louis Stevenson."

"Really?" Dawn was surprised. "I'd have thought you'd be more interested in Steven King."

Shane grinned. "I'll bet there will be enough people doing *him.* I figure that picking a classic author can't hurt. Sucking up pays off sometimes. And I do like Stevenson, so he's a logical choice. How about you?"

"I haven't read much of his stuff," Dawn admitted.

"No, I mean, have you decided what you're doing?"

"I'm still trying to," she said and pulled the book from her bag to show to Shane. "Mr. Belding seems to think this would give me some ideas."

Shane looked at the book. *"A Plague of Pixies?"* he said incredulously. "By William vande Water? You've got to be joking!" He turned it over to read the write-up on the back.

Smiling, Dawn told him, "Mr. Belding says that there was this village he stayed in that was supposed to be a gateway to the magical kingdom of fairies and whatever. He knows I like fantasy."

"Really?" asked Vince, abruptly looking up from his book. "Like what?"

"Diana Wynne Jones is my favorite," Dawn said.

"Yeah, she's okay. Tried any Esther Friesner?"

"Balbec," said Shane suddenly, reading from the back of the book cover. A frown creased his brow. "I've heard that name before."

"It's where the Beldings stayed on their honeymoon," Dawn informed him. "You probably heard him mention it."

"No, that's not it," Shane said slowly. "Vince, does it ring a bell with you?"

"Balbec?" Vince giggled. "Maybe it should be *Bell*bec."

"Thank you, Einstein." Shane shook his head. "I can't place it. But I will." He offered her the book back. "That looks pretty wild. Maybe Mr. Belding will let me borrow it when you're done with it."

"Probably," she agreed. She slid it back into her

bag. The book had served its purpose—to break the ice—and she promptly forgot it. "So, are you going to be busy on the project all week?"

Shane gave her a shy smile. "I could take an evening off," he offered. "If *you* could, that is."

"I'll force myself," she replied with a grin. "Maybe tomorrow?"

"Cool," said Vince, raising his head again. "Is it going to be a foursome?" Seeing Dawn's blank expression, he added, "You know, with Carolyn as well? She's cute in a weird sort of way."

Dawn felt like groaning. She didn't want Vince along at all, really. "You'll have to ask her yourself," she replied.

"No problemo." He returned to his book. Shane simply shrugged. Obviously even he couldn't get through to Vince some days.

Carolyn joined them about ten minutes later when practice broke up. "I think I wore off my fingerprints," she complained. She held up her left hand, and Dawn could see where she'd been pressing the strings, leaving red marks across the tips of each finger. "I need a break badly!"

"Tomorrow night," said Vince abruptly.

"What?" asked Carolyn, puzzled.

"The four of us are going out," he explained.

"Um, Vince, you were supposed to *ask,"* Shane said hastily.

"Oh. *Are* we going out?"

Carolyn glared at him. "Two words," she snapped. "No way."

Vince didn't seem to be bothered. "Another night?" he asked hopefully. "Wednesday? Thursday?"

"When hell freezes over," Carolyn informed him. "And not a day sooner."

"Okay." Vince returned to his book.

Carolyn rolled her eyes at Dawn. "Let's get out of here," she said. "Before my brain goes on vacation." She stormed off toward the exit.

Shane gave Vince a despairing look. "Way to go, knucklehead," he said.

"She likes me," Vince announced happily.

Dawn wondered if he'd lost touch with reality. "How do you figure?" she asked.

"She's the first girl I've ever asked out who hasn't threatened to barf all over me," Vince explained. "She *must* like me."

"Dream on," Dawn muttered. She threw a quick smile at Shane. "Tomorrow," she said. "Just the two of us?"

Shane glanced at Vince and nodded emphatically. "I promise."

Dawn nodded, then chased after Carolyn, catching her before she made it out of the auditorium. "How did the practice go?"

Carolyn gave her a sly grin. "I'd say you made better music than me for once. So you got Shane to ask you out finally?"

"Yeah."

"That's great." Carolyn stopped and glared at her. "But even for you, I am *not* going to be seen with Vince Holloway. No way, understand?"

"Sure," agreed Dawn.

"Say it like you mean it!" begged Carolyn. Then she pointed across the parking lot. "Hey, isn't that your mom's Lumina?"

"Yes. I guess she got off work early." Then another thought struck her. "I just hope it's not because she has bad news." She didn't want to think of that, but she had no choice. By the time she reached her mother's car, she was worried enough to ask immediately: "Is Candy okay?"

Dawn's mother nodded. "I hope so. But I did come to tell you that Dr. Calfa has finally decided to sedate her so she can get some sleep—and, hopefully, rest."

"But she's okay?" persisted Dawn.

Dr. Jacobs sighed. "She's asleep now," she admitted. "But I'm not sure she's getting any real rest. She's still dreaming. Her brain is a hive of activity. If it doesn't slow down soon, Candy's brain may stop altogether."

"Just like Jesse's—" Dawn whispered, appalled.

CHAPTER 6

There was a loud rap on Vince's bedroom door. "Bedtime, young man," his mother called through it. "Put your book down and get some rest!"

With a sigh, Vince marked his page and placed the volume on his night table. "Okay, Mom," he called. He switched off his light and snuggled down into the sheets. "Good night."

He'd really been enjoying this latest book, and his mind was buzzing with ideas. It was another UFO sighting and government coverup paperback, and Vince loved those. He was absolutely convinced that flying saucers were real and that aliens constantly visited the earth. He was equally certain that the government knew about their visits but kept quiet for their own dark and selfish reasons.

Vince peered out of the small gaps in the blinds over his bedroom window. Tiny bars of light came through, and he could see one or two stars. He desperately wished he could see a UFO personally; so far, he'd seen zilch. It seemed unfair that so many people could spot them and he, for all his faith in their existence, had never seen a single one.

Well, one day, it was bound to happen.

He dozed off, his mind filled with thoughts of extraterrestrial contact and beings from beyond.

Vince awoke, disoriented and puzzled. There was something very odd. He was lying on his back but couldn't move. It was as if he were paralyzed somehow. Despite the fact that this should have terrified him, he felt a deep sense of calm. He lay there, peacefully, trying to work out what was happening. After a moment he realized that he wasn't hearing any sounds. There should be the soft ticking of his alarm clock, at least, or the rustling of trees outside.

Nothing. Not a sound. Not even the soft sound of his own heartbeat.

Am I dead? he wondered. He'd read about strange near-death experiences where people didn't know they were dead. But he was certain that this wasn't the case. For one thing, though he couldn't move, he was still breathing. He could feel his chest rising and falling. Had he simply gone deaf then? Was he having some kind of seizure or something? After all, not being able to move should scare him. Why was he reacting so oddly?

Then, through his closed eyelids, he could make out a very faint glow. It had to be bright if he could see it with his eyes closed. It seemed to be flickering. Was the house on fire maybe? Possibly the oil burner was giving off carbon monoxide? He'd heard that this could kill. No, that wasn't right. It made you sick—it didn't paralyze you. And there was no smell of smoke. If the smoke detector was blaring, he couldn't hear it—but, then, he couldn't hear anything.

Concentrating really hard, he finally managed to get his eyelids open. For a moment he lay there, relieved that he hadn't gone blind as well as deaf. Then he saw the play of lights on his ceiling. The main color was a sort of silvery glow, but mixed with it was a warm red and a bluish green fuzziness. The three colors were distinct and moving about as if they were spinning. Vince realized that the light was flooding his room from outside the bedroom window. Whatever was causing the light was in the backyard, which didn't make a lot of sense. It definitely meant that the house wasn't on fire, though.

The yard was pretty small, and he couldn't imagine what might be out there causing lights like this. Maybe it was the house behind, the one owned by the Brubakers? Were they having a party or something, and the lights were from their house? But it had to be the middle of the night! And it didn't explain why Vince couldn't hear anything or move.

The lights suddenly began to whirl about in a mad dance on the ceiling, faster and faster. Then Vince realized that something even stranger was happening. His body became very light. Was he having some kind of out-of-body experience? He'd read of cases like those, where a person suddenly finds himself floating in the air above his own sleeping body. However, his spirit wasn't leaving his body—it was his body that was growing lighter and—

Then he gently floated up from his bed, until he was about four feet above it. He still couldn't move anything but his eyes, but the calm feeling within him persisted. Whatever was happening to him, he felt certain that it was nothing bad. This was the weirdest thing that had ever happened, but he felt very peaceful.

Gradually, he spun around so his feet were now pointed toward the window. The blinds were still down, but he could see through the slats that the lights shining on the ceiling were definitely coming from the backyard. Several bright sources were out there, spinning wildly, sending shafts of light into the room. Vince didn't know what was making him float or move, but the odd force started to tug him toward the window.

Was he going to crash into it? He knew he should be worried, but still the feeling of utter peace comforted him. As his feet reached the blinds, he felt them pass right through the wooden slats as if they and the house had suddenly ceased to have any physical presence. His body slipped through the blinds and windowpane as easily as it had slipped through the bed sheets and the air.

He was outside now. It was definitely the middle of the night. Overhead the stars glittered, unmasked by clouds. Vince felt neither cold nor the slightest breath of wind. He still could hear nothing. But he could see—and *what* he could see!

There was no doubt—it was a flying saucer, hovering over the backyard, blotting out some of the stars. The lights that spun and flashed were part of the craft's base, which was quickly rotating. The saucer was, well, saucer shaped. He could see only the underside. It appeared to be about thirty feet across, and in the dead center of the spinning section was an open hatchway of some sort. Vince floated through the air until he was directly beneath the hole, and then he felt himself rising up into the space beyond.

Excitement filled him: He was going to meet the alien creatures who must have piloted this spaceship across billions of miles of space! This was incredible! It was his greatest wish, and it was about to be fulfilled.

Once he was inside the hatch, he stopped rising. There was a shimmer of movement, and Vince realized that the hatch had closed. It cut off the spinning, dancing lights, leaving only a warm, silvery glow in the room in which he found himself.

The walls were semitransparent, a silvery color that

seemed to glow from within. In the walls and the ceiling were twisted squiggles, thin and long, like veins under the skin or the capillaries of a leaf. These were slightly darker than the walls, making the place appear organic. It was as if the walls were somehow alive, as if he were floating inside a gigantic brain. Totally wild!

He felt something under his back. A table or a couch had risen from the floor, it appeared, and was now supporting him. The floating sensation stopped, and he regained his normal weight. He was still unable to move, however, and could only lie still on the table.

There was a slight movement off to one side and then another. He couldn't make it out because he couldn't turn his head. Then it came closer, and if he had been able to move, he would have gasped and stared.

It was one of the alien beings. He could only see it from about the middle of its chest up, but it seemed smaller than a fully grown human. It couldn't have been as much as five feet tall. It was a silvery gray color, but it was impossible to tell if it was naked or wearing a form-fitting bodysuit. There were no marks on the alien's body at all, nor was there any sign of hair. The head was large in proportion to the body, and it had a very high, rounded skull. There was a small mouth, barely more than a slash in its face. Above this were two even smaller vertical slashes that had to be the being's nostrils. Above high cheekbones were the alien's eyes. They were huge, easily three times the size of Vince's, and completely black. There was no sign of an iris, as if the being's eyes were just huge pupils. The eyes gave the alien a sad, wistful expression.

It was impossible to tell what the creature felt or thought, though. Its expression didn't change as it moved about the couch on which Vince lay. Its arms were long and very thin. In one hand it held some sort of instrument—wishbone shaped, again in a silvery metallic color—that was softly glowing. The alien was passing the two prongs of this wishbone over every part of Vince's body while examining some sort of screen in its other hand. Vince realized he was being given a medical checkup. After a few moments the alien moved away.

Vince wanted to call out, to ask the being to come back, but he couldn't. There was so much he wanted to know, but he was incapable of asking anything. This was the chance of a lifetime—meeting real live creatures from another planet! But all he could do was lie there. There were so many questions these beings could answer! Scientific, spiritual, and just plain curious ones! But without the power to speak, there was nothing Vince could do.

A moment later the creature returned. Vince assumed that it was the same one, though it might have been a second one absolutely identical to the first. There was no way to tell. It was holding a different piece of equipment, one that looked like a calculator with a needle attached. The alien held this close to Vince's leg and then stared down at Vince.

No words were spoken, but Vince was certain he'd heard "Do not fear." It had to be some kind of telepathy! This was incredible. And he didn't feel at all afraid. He couldn't speak to tell the small alien that he wasn't afraid, but the being seemed to understand.

It moved the needle close to Vince's right thigh. There was a sharp puncturing feeling, and then a terrible fire grew in Vince's leg. The pain was overwhelming, and he lost consciousness then.

When he recovered, he found himself back in bed at home. The paralysis was gone, and his hearing had returned. He could make out the soft ticking of his clock and the sighing and gurgling of water in the heating pipes.

He'd been returned home while unconscious! It had been an awesome experience—he, Vince Holloway, had been contacted by alien beings! He sat up and slipped out of bed. As he started to stand, his right leg gave way and he fell back onto the bed. There was a sharp pain in his thigh. He switched on the bedside light, grimacing. Pulling down his pajama bottoms, he examined the area in the low light. There was a red rash on the thigh, like the bite from a mosquito. Touching it, he discovered it was a little tender and there was a slight bump.

He'd heard of incidents in which people had been taken aboard flying saucers and small pieces of some alien metal was injected under their skin. Nobody quite knew why, but it was presumably some sort of alien tagging system that enabled them to track their subjects. And, maybe, to contact him again someday!

Vince pulled his bottoms back up, and on his second attempt managed to stand up. He walked slowly to his window, his leg feeling better with each step he took. He opened the blinds and stared out.

He hadn't really expected the UFO to be there still, and it wasn't. There was the faint glow of dawn on the horizon, but nothing at all to show what had happened to him. It didn't bother Vince. He *knew* what had happened. Excitement filled his whole being. At long last, he had met an alien being!

Okay, he didn't know exactly what the alien had wanted with him, and he really didn't *know* a whole lot. It had been an incredible experience, but he hadn't learned much. Still, he now knew from personal experience that there *were* alien beings.

Just wait till the guys at school heard about this!

CHAPTER 7

Dawn knew that she should have been feeling excited, but she simply couldn't work up the proper enthusiasm. Even though tonight was to be her first date with Shane, something she'd dreamed about for months, she was depressed. It was hard to think about enjoying herself while Candy was still so ill.

"No change?" asked Carolyn when the two friends met outside school on Tuesday morning.

"None," replied Dawn with a sigh. "She's still out, and she's still dreaming." Dawn shook her head. "Mom says they've flown in experts from New York and Los Angeles, and still everybody's baffled. They can't figure it out."

Carolyn tried to smile. "Don't they always say it's darkest before the dawn or something dumb like that?" She put an arm around her friend's shoulder. "She'll be okay, Dawn. She's got to be."

"I'd like to believe it," Dawn replied. "The faintest glimmer of hope would be enough. But there's *nothing.*"

Carolyn nodded. "Well, *there's* something. Shane Morrow, to be exact. And he looks happy enough."

Dawn turned and saw Shane hurrying over to them. He looked happy and anxious at the same time. "Hi," he said a little breathlessly. "Tonight still on?"

"Yes," Dawn replied.

Carolyn glared at her. "Hey, at least *try* to sound like you're looking forward to it, girl," she snapped.

Dawn blushed. "I'm sorry. I *am* looking forward to it. It's just that . . ."

Shane nodded his understanding. "Can't get Candy out of your thoughts. You want to postpone going out till she's better?"

"No," Dawn answered quickly. "I'll be more cheerful tonight, I promise."

Carolyn gave a groan. "Speaking of cheerful, here comes a whole bucketload of the stuff. What is with this guy?" She'd spotted Vince hurrying over, the biggest, goofiest grin on his face.

"Maybe his computer had puppies," Dawn muttered. Shane tried to stifle a giggle.

"Hey, guys!" Vince yelled. "You'll never guess what

happened to me last night!" He caught up with them, puffing and looking like he'd run all the way to school.

"You had a personality transplant with an onion?" guessed Carolyn.

"No," Vince answered, apparently not having heard her. "I was abducted by a UFO!"

"Ow," muttered Carolyn. "Why didn't they *keep* you? Couldn't they stand you either?"

Dawn stared at Vince. "You're joking, right?"

"No, *really,*" insisted Vince. "I was taken aboard a flying saucer last night."

Carolyn rolled her eyes. "Either you've developed a sense of humor, which I would have sworn was beyond you, or you've seriously flipped out. Either way, I'm out of here."

Dawn grabbed her arm before she could leave. She stared at Vince and realized that he was almost hopping up and down in excitement. "You're *serious?"*

"Am I ever!" Vince's grin couldn't have been wider without splitting his face. He then proceeded to tell them everything he'd experienced, despite Carolyn's intermittent groans. His hands flew about as he gestured and acted out what he'd been though. "Then I woke up in my own bed," he finished.

"Where you were the whole time," Carolyn snapped. "Vince, you were *dreaming."*

"No, I wasn't!" He sounded hurt by the accusation.

Dawn could feel sorry for him, but she couldn't really accept his wild story. "You *must* have been dreaming," she said gently.

"Why don't you believe me?" Vince asked, pathetic and puzzled.

Shane sighed. "Vince, you've got to realize that this is kind of . . . weird."

"Right," added Carolyn. "Even for you, this is major league weird. And you're not the person I'd exactly consider the most stable member of the community. The San Andreas fault is more stable than your mental state."

"But it happened!" Vince insisted. "Honest, it did!"

Dawn said, "Vince, *maybe* it did. But there's no proof. You must realize that people aren't going to accept your story without some sort of evidence. It's just too wild."

Vince stared at the three of them, confusion and disappointment written all over his face. Then he lit up with a huge smile again. "But I've *got* proof!" he said. "I told you, the alien doctor or whatever he was put something into my leg! It left a mark, and there's got to be something under it. I'll show you." He started to reach for his belt.

Carolyn gasped and grabbed his arm. "Vince, the school yard is *not* the place to drop your pants! Good grief, don't you have *any* brains left in your head?"

"Uh, yeah," he agreed, flushing as he realized what he had almost done in his excitement. "But that's proof, isn't it?"

"If there's anything there, it *might* be," agreed Dawn.

Vince was on a roll now. "Your mom's a doctor, isn't she?"

"Yes," agreed Dawn cautiously, wondering what he was getting at.

"Well, she could X-ray my leg and that would show what's in there, wouldn't it?"

Carolyn snorted. "She should X-ray your skull to see if there's anything in there at all."

Dawn didn't know what to say. She didn't want to involve her mother in this, but at the same time it was obvious that Vince was desperate for something to back up his claim of being abducted by a UFO. "I'll tell you what," she said finally. "I'll call her at work and see if she'll consider it. If she says no, that's it, though. Okay?"

It didn't seem to get through to Vince that she might refuse. "Terrific," he agreed. "After school today? No time like the present."

Dawn winced; it meant her date with Shane would probably be off! Shane realized what she was thinking and shrugged.

"It's up to you," he said. "But it means a lot to Vince."

"I'm the one who needs her head tested," Dawn groaned. "Okay, I'll see what Mom has to say." She could just imagine what the response would be: "This flaky friend of yours wants his leg X-rayed to see if there's an alien wildlife tag in it?" But Vince looked so pathetically grateful that she couldn't bring herself to tell him to get lost.

Dawn called her mother at lunchtime and managed

to get through fairly quickly. "It's a slow day," Dr. Jacobs told her. "Thank goodness. What's wrong, love?"

"Um, I don't quite know how to ask this," Dawn admitted. "But one of the guys at school thinks he was abducted from his bed by aliens last night."

Dr. Jacobs laughed. "What's this, cheer-up-Mother day?"

"No, he really believes it. He's a bit weird sometimes, but this is further than he's ever gone before. Anyway, he says the aliens put something into his leg, and he thinks that if you X-ray him, it'll prove his story." There was a pause, and Dawn wondered if she was going to get told off for wasting her mother's time.

"Well," Mom said finally, "that's certainly different. I'll tell you what. Come down with this—friend after school. If there's no great demand, I'll see what I can do. To be honest, we could all do with something to make us smile. Trying to find a UFO fragment in his leg might raise a few spirits around here."

Dawn rang off and went to find Vince. She wasn't too surprised to discover he'd cornered Carolyn and was again trying to get her to go out with him. Shane was there also, an amused smile on his face.

"Save me," Carolyn called to Dawn. "Knock him out, please. Or, better still, knock *me* out and put me out of my misery!"

"Sorry," Dawn replied, grinning slightly. "I left my knock-out drops in my other skirt pocket."

"And you call yourself my friend," complained Carolyn. She turned back to Vince. "I don't want to go out with you," she said slowly. "I'd sooner feed myself to the sharks than see you socially. Do you understand?"

"Ah, you're just kidding," Vince answered.

Reality and Vince were obviously not sharing the same planet, Dawn realized. She was more convinced than ever that Vince must have dreamed his close encounter with aliens. Still, she *might* just be wrong. "I spoke to my mother," she said, saving Carolyn from further harassment. "She says to stop by and she'll try to get the X ray done. No promises, though."

"All right!" crowed Vince happily. "That'll prove I'm right!"

"Or," Carolyn said darkly, "it'll prove you're wrong. Hasn't that occurred to you?"

"No," Vince answered, puzzled. "I know I'm not wrong."

Dawn shook her head in amazement. Clearly Vince was convinced his experience had been real. She just hoped that the reality of what turned up wouldn't break his heart.

"Some first date," muttered Shane apologetically.

Dawn glanced around the hospital corridor where they were waiting. Carolyn had reluctantly accompanied them, but it had taken a lot of pleading on Dawn's part to accomplish it. Carolyn was terrified that Vince would be convinced that this meant they were doubling. Dawn wished she could reassure Carolyn, but she suspected her friend was right.

Dr. Jacobs had actually managed to get the X-ray

technicians to agree to do the shot of Vince's leg. It was being developed right now. Dawn was sure her mom was correct, and that everyone was just hoping to get a laugh out of the whole business. It wasn't hard to see that they didn't get a whole lot to grin at in the emergency room.

Carolyn had refused to wait with them while the X ray was being developed. "I couldn't take being with Vince that long," she admitted. Instead, she'd gone upstairs to see if she could look in on Candy. Dawn and Shane had been forced to sit and listen to Vince's theories about what he'd gone through on the flying saucer.

"I'm sure it's some kind of communicator they've implanted in my leg," he explained. "This way, they can always find me if they need me. And I'm sure they will."

"Oh, I don't know," Shane replied. "It sounds to me more like the kind of thing that scientists do with wildlife—you know, sort of like a radio collar or whatever. Maybe as far as the aliens are concerned, the human race is not really that intelligent."

"Especially if they picked *you* as a sample," Dawn muttered.

"No," Vince replied, treating Shane's outrageous suggestion with full gravity. "They are bound to recognize the intelligence and dignity of the human race. They must see what we have accomplished. I know they've been monitoring our space shots, you know. There are several cases of them shadowing space shuttle missions."

"You've got to stop subscribing to the *National Enquirer,"* Dawn told him. "They're the only people who believe this stuff."

"No, it's true," Vince insisted. "The government is covering up the truth for their own motives, but we who have been contacted know the truth: Alien visitors are real."

"It all sounds too bizarre to me," Shane admitted. "I mean—kidnapping you from your bed to perform a couple of medical tests on you, stick something in your leg, and then return you? If you ask me, it doesn't make *them* sound very intelligent."

Vince shook his head. "Of course we can't understand why they do things; they're a vastly more advanced species than we are. Their actions are bound to puzzle us."

"Give it up," Dawn advised Shane. "He's clearly immune to logical reasoning."

"I was starting to suspect that," agreed Shane.

Thankfully, before Vince could explain any more of his theories, Dawn's mother came out of the X-ray department. She held a large negative in her hand and wore a puzzled expression on her face.

"What's the verdict?" asked Vince eagerly. "Does it prove I'm right?"

"Well, not exactly," Dr. Jacobs told him. She held the X ray up, and Vince stared at it, awe on his face. Dawn and Shane crowded in for a look. The length of the femur and the tip of the kneecap were quite clear. A smoky area surrounded the bones, showing where the tissue, muscle, and skin lay. Dawn's mother tapped a part of the X ray midway up the bone. "This is where the redness and swelling on your thigh occur," she explained to Vince. "As you can see, there *is* something there, close to the bone."

"I told you! I told you!" Vince was almost dancing with joy.

"But it's not metal or anything obviously artificial," Dr. Jacobs added quickly and loudly. "If it was, it would be much brighter on the X ray, like the bones are."

Dawn could see that there was a tear-shaped patch of milkiness where her mother was pointing. "So, what is it?" she asked.

Her mother shrugged. "Some kind of cyst, I'd say. Probably benign, but there's no evidence of scarring, as there would be if something had been implanted in Vince's leg. We could do more tests, maybe take a sample."

"No, there's no need," Vince said happily. "I *told* you there was something there, and that proves it. I was right all the time! I *was* taken aboard a spaceship."

Dr. Jacobs was about to object, but Dawn gripped her mother's arm. "There's no point," she said. "Vince *wants* to believe it was real. It doesn't matter what you tell him, he'll only hear what he wants to hear." She gestured to the picture. "You're sure it's not anything to worry about, though?"

Her mother shook her head. "As I said, probably a cyst. It'll most likely dissolve. If it doesn't go in a few days, make him go to see his doctor, okay?" She smiled at Shane. "There's no point in asking Vince to promise, so I'll ask you instead."

"I know what you mean, Dr. Jacobs," Shane said. Vince had his fist clenched in a victory salute and was hopping about with a blissful expression on his face. "I promise to follow up on this."

"Good." Dawn's mother stared at Vince and shook her head. "Maybe I should have him take a mental test, but I'd be afraid to find out what's going on in his head."

"Don't worry; he's harmless," Shane assured her. "And you've made him a very happy guy today."

"Which means," said Dawn, "we'll never hear the end of this. He believes he's been singled out for some special purpose, and he's determined to discover what it is."

"Even if it costs the rest of us our sanity," agreed Shane.

CHAPTER 8

"What have I done to deserve this?" asked Carolyn theatrically. "I've studied hard, been good to my kid brother, practiced my violin daily, and I'm nice to animals. What have I done to deserve Vince Holloway haunting me?"

"He likes you," Dawn replied without much sympathy. "He thinks you're gorgeous, witty, intelligent, and romantic."

"All of which are perfectly true," agreed Carolyn shamelessly. "But he also thinks I'm madly in love with him, which is *definitely* not."

"Four out of five isn't bad," Dawn answered.

"It is when you consider the fifth."

"Why don't you simply tell him you're not interested?" Dawn asked her friend. They were heading across the parking lot toward the school Wednesday morning.

"Are you kidding?" Carolyn stopped short, astonished. "I've been telling him nothing but! Vince is completely impervious. He just thinks I'm playing hard to get because I don't want him to think I'm a pushover. Everything I say or do becomes twisted logic in what he laughingly calls a mind and comes out all wrong. If I pulled a gun out and shot him, he'd be convinced it was so no other girl could have him." Carolyn shook her head and continued walking. "Honest, Dawn, he's driving me crazy. You're my friend. Help me!"

"How?" asked Dawn. "He won't listen to a word I say either."

"Well, if you were really my friend," Carolyn said, "you'd make a play for him. Make him date *you* instead!" She stopped dead in her tracks. "Oh, no!"

There, just ahead of them, were Shane and Vince. Vince was chattering away, gesturing wildly. He hadn't seen the two girls yet, but it was only a matter of seconds.

"Quick!" hissed Carolyn, clutching Dawn's arm. "Let's head for the side entrance. Let's play hooky. Let's do anything, but do it *fast.*"

Much as Dawn wanted to be with Shane, she couldn't resist Carolyn's pleas. "Okay." Quickly, they changed direction and headed for the other doorway. Dawn glanced over her shoulder once and saw that Vince was still talking up a storm. He hadn't even noticed them. She hoped that Shane wouldn't mind bearing the brunt of Vince's monologue. While she wasn't quite as averse to Vince as Carolyn, Dawn wasn't thrilled about meeting him. It was the one drawback to being with Shane.

"Safe!" exclaimed Carolyn once they were inside the building. "Thank you, God!" She smiled at Dawn. "Got to go to music," she said. "Catch you next period, okay?" Then she shot off down the corridor.

Dawn sighed and shook her head before starting off for English lit. She arrived early, so she pulled out the book Mr. Belding had lent her and started to flip through it.

The teacher was right—it was a fascinating story. All nonsense and rampant superstition, of course. According to the first few pages—all she had time to read—the small village of Balbec was invaded by the citizens of Fairyland in the late sixteenth century. Pixies, goblins, ogres, and other mythical creatures were seen by the inhabitants of Balbec almost nightly. It was reported there was a door between the magical kingdom and Balbec in the surrounding mountains, and some people were actually taken in through the solid rock of the mountainside to visit the kingdom of the Fair Folk.

Dawn loved the idea of walking through a wall of rock into a magic kingdom even though there was no way it could be true. But in the Middle Ages there were people who believed implicitly in such tales. Then again, there were still people like that nowadays —people who sincerely believed that Elvis was still alive or that Bigfoot existed.

Even people who believed they had been abducted by space aliens! Vince would have been right at home in the Middle Ages.

Right on cue, Vince and Shane walked into the classroom. Dawn slipped the book back into her bag and smiled at Shane. He smiled back, then rolled his eyes at her over Vince's shoulder. Vince was still talking.

"Then there was the Bouchard case in 1968," he said, "where a man was knocked out by a bright light from the sky and paralyzed for days. Then—"

"What *is* he going on about?" Dawn asked, puzzled.

"UFO sightings that resulted in strange behaviors," Shane explained. "Apparently he sat up all night researching them."

"Why?" Dawn thought that even for Vince this was going to extremes.

"Because," Vince replied quickly, "I think that's what happened to Candace. She was another person the aliens attempted to contact, but something went wrong, and she was left in a weird paralysis. There are lots of precedents—"

"Don't start on them again!" Shane begged. "My head's spinning already."

"Besides," Dawn added, "that's not Candy's problem."

"She's flaked out at the hospital, right?" Vince asked.

"No," Dawn told him gently. "She's been drugged to make her sleep. She couldn't get to sleep. And I think if she'd seen a flying saucer or been abducted, she'd have mentioned it to somebody—like me. But she certainly never said anything of the kind."

"Oh." For a second Vince actually shut up. Then he brightened. "Maybe she repressed the memory. It happens a lot in UFO contact cases, you know. People only recall being contacted after hypnosis or therapy. If she's had some sort of mental problem, that could be the reason, you know."

"Vince, I think *you're* the one who needs therapy." Dawn didn't want to be cruel, but she was losing patience with his theories. "Not everyone with a problem has met aliens, you know."

"Well, it's just something you should consider," he insisted.

Mr. Belding walked into the room at that point. For a moment Vince kept on chattering, but then he managed to restrain himself and pay attention to the lesson. Shane gave Dawn a sympathetic smile and patted her hand.

Dawn was glad to be able to focus on something other than Candy or Vince for a while. What puzzled her, though, was that there was an itchy sort of feeling in the back of her mind. Something was trying to take shape, she knew, but it wasn't quite coming into focus. She forced herself to forget about it for the class and tried to pay attention. Her wandering thoughts weren't helped by the fact that Vince's pent-up energy had been channeled from chattering to scratching. Every few seconds he scraped at the back of his neck until it was red and almost bleeding.

After a while even the teacher noticed. "Vince," Mr. Belding said in a kindly tone. "Is there a problem?"

"Uh? What?" Vince sat bolt upright, obviously striving to focus his mind. Andrea and a few of the other students snickered. "No, sir, no problem."

"Oh." The teacher raised an eyebrow. "I thought you might have fleas or something."

Vince caught his hand as he was about to scratch his neck again. Blushing, he slammed it down on the desk. "Uh, no, sir. No fleas." The snickering was a little louder.

"Good." The teacher glanced around the room and the giggling stopped. "Right, now, on page forty-three . . ."

Dawn tried to concentrate on the lesson but soon was aware that Vince was having problems. He was clearly fighting the urge to scratch again. His fingers started to twitch, and a moment later, he was tapping them on his desk. It was very irritating, and after a minute, Mr. Belding placed his book down once again.

"Vince," he said, "maybe you had better start drinking decaf." There was a general laugh, and Vince turned red again.

With a huge effort, he stopped drumming his fingers. "Sorry, sir," he apologized again. There was a tick in his cheek.

"Maybe you'd better go get a drink of water," the teacher suggested. "It may make you feel better."

"Yeah, thanks," Vince agreed and promptly bolted from the room. He didn't return for the remaining ten minutes of class.

As soon as the period was over, Dawn hurried off to find Carolyn to go to PE when Dawn caught up with her. "Vince is acting really weird this morning," she said.

"How can you tell?" asked Carolyn. "He's *always* weird."

"Yes," Dawn agreed. "But even he has limits. Today he seems to be freaking out. I think he's letting his supposed abduction go right to his head."

"That's because there's not a lot in there already," Carolyn argued. "It's all alone up there, so it's bound to become a mania with him. Oh, great—speaking of manias . . ." She gestured down the corridor.

Vince was standing in the doorway of a room they had to pass, talking animatedly to Shane, who acted very uncomfortable. Vince was scratching the back of his left hand now. His right foot was tapping the floor.

"Come on, Vince," Shane was saying as the girls passed. "Let's go inside. You're starting to bug me."

"Bug you?" Vince stared at him blankly. Then he blinked several times rapidly. As Dawn wondered what was going on in his strange little mind he abruptly screamed. Dawn winced, deafened by the sheer volume and terror in the voice.

"Jeez!" yelped Carolyn.

"Bugs!" Vince howled, scratching at his skin like crazy. "All over me! Bugs!" He screamed again, ripping at his skin so hard he left bloody scratches. "Get them off me! They're eating me alive!"

Dawn suddenly realized what that itching in the back of her mind was trying to tell her. "Vince!" she said, almost in a panic. "Calm down! You're sick!" She tried to grab hold of him, but he twisted away, still screaming.

"Don't touch me!" he howled. "You're all covered with bugs, too! Can't you see them? Can't you feel them?"

Dawn made another dive for him. "Stop it, Vince!"

He dodged her, then whirled and ran down the corridor, knocking aside anybody in his way. He was screaming and scratching at his skin as he ran.

Dawn shot a quick, worried look at Carolyn and Shane, who were both stunned. "It's the sickness," she gasped. "Vince has what Candy and Jesse had. He's hallucinating! We've got to stop him!"

Her friends caught on, and together they sprinted after Vince. More students were pushed out of the way as they plowed after the fleeing lunatic. Dawn had no idea where he was heading, and she suspected that neither did Vince. Shane's inadvertent comment about bugging him had set off some kind of nightmare in his mind. He must be scared of insects, she guessed, and was now convinced he was being devoured by them. In his panic, he wasn't paying any attention to what he was doing.

He slammed out of the main doors, still screaming and ripping at his skin. Dawn, Carolyn, and Shane were just seconds behind him, but Vince was drawing speed from his terror. He was halfway across the parking lot already, heading for the main road.

"Damn!" gasped Shane as he ran. "He's not watching where he's going! Vince! Wait up!" Shane was a faster sprinter than the girls and pulled away from them.

Carolyn clearly saw that Shane was right. "Vince!" she yelled. "Stop! I love you!" She gave a slight grin as she passed Dawn. "I'm going to regret that later, but it might stop him—Vince! I want you!"

Even that didn't get through the panic that had gripped Vince. With Shane hot on his heels, Vince ran straight out onto the main road.

Dawn stopped dead, terrified and shocked. Vince hadn't paused despite the traffic. Even though the cars were going slower than normal because of the school zone, they were still doing almost thirty. Vince stumbled right into the path of a car, not even seeing it. It slammed into him, brakes screeching.

Vince cannoned off the hood of the car and was flung across the road—directly into the path of a pickup heading the opposite way. The driver tried to brake and swerve to avoid Vince, but it was too late. There was a sickening thud as the car collided with

Vince. His shattered body was tossed up again and landed with a nauseating *splat* beside the sidewalk.

Shane and Dawn remained fixed to their spots. Carolyn gave a piercing scream and collapsed in a dead faint.

Blood trickled from the obviously dead body of Vince Holloway and stained the road.

CHAPTER 9

Dawn asked sympathetically: "How are you feeling?"

Shaking her head slightly, Carolyn replied, "Lousy. Which is a definite improvement." She stroked idly at the sheet covering her in her bed, clearly at a loss for words. "I can't believe I fainted."

Dawn smiled sadly and patted Carolyn's hand. "I can't believe I *didn't,*" she said. "I felt like I was going to, though."

"Yeah." Carolyn was obviously reliving her memories of the accident. "It was so awful, wasn't it? Just to watch helplessly as Vince was killed like that."

"There wasn't anything else we could do," Dawn replied. She felt terrible about Vince and almost as bad for her friend. After the cars had hit Vince, Shane and Dawn had rushed over to his broken body, but it was absolutely clear that poor Vince was already dead. Fighting not to throw up, Dawn had returned to check on Carolyn. To her relief, her friend's pulse was strong. She had simply fainted.

Someone must have called the police and an ambulance, because the next thing Dawn recalled was hearing the wail of their sirens. Dawn then felt hands on her shoulders, and she looked up in surprise to see Andrea Calloway—without her usual snide grin.

"Let me help you," Andrea offered.

"What?" Dawn was still very confused, her emotions raging.

Andrea gestured at Carolyn. "We can't leave her on the sidewalk," she pointed out. "The two of us can get her back inside the school, though." She was making sense. Dawn nodded. Together, they each took an arm and formed a firefighter's chair to carry Carolyn into the nurse's office. Dawn was quite surprised by Andrea's concern and sensible attitude. It was not at all like the usual Andrea. Somewhat embarrassed, Andrea had gone off as soon as Carolyn was inside.

Waiting for Carolyn's mother to come and get her, Dawn watched the police and paramedics arrive. They couldn't do much more than load Vince's body into the ambulance and remove it. A uniformed officer questioned Shane and a few other students. Dawn watched from the infirmary window, wondering if the police would talk to her and Carolyn as well. But they didn't.

Shane had stopped by, looking concerned, pale, and a little sick. "I called my folks," he told her. "I've got to go see Vince's folks. They're going to be shattered by this news. I know I'm shattered."

"Take care of yourself," Dawn told him. He and Vince had been very close for years, she knew, and Shane was almost shaking. He was probably going home to have a good cry. Dawn wished she could cry right then. Not that she'd been terribly fond of Vince, but his death had been horrible. She'd have been appalled to see even a stranger killed like that. But for it to be someone she knew, even a pest, was worse. It had to be tearing Shane apart. She gave him a kiss on the cheek. "Call me if you want someone to talk to tonight," she said.

"Thanks." With haunted eyes, he left the nurse's office.

Dawn needed to cry to relieve the emotional pressure building within herself. But it was no use—she was in a state of shock. The floods would come later. She sat with Carolyn—still out to the world—until Mrs. Rice arrived. Together, they had taken Carolyn home and put her to bed. Dawn had filled Mrs. Rice in about the events of the morning.

She realized with some shock that it was still before noon. It felt as if the day had been going on forever.

Dawn had been there when Carolyn awoke. Pale and shaking, her friend managed a weak smile. Then, wincing, she said, "He's dead, isn't he?"

"Yes." There was no gentle way to tell her.

Carolyn nodded, sniffed, and then burst into tears. That started Dawn going, too, as all her emotions crashed at once. Clinging to each other, they cried themselves stupid. Finally, after using up most of a box of tissues, they settled down.

Feeling mildly better now that the tears had washed out much of her pent-up stress, Dawn was able to speak. So was Carolyn.

"I feel like such a witch," Carolyn admitted. "I was so horrible to Vince, even if it didn't sink in. And now he's dead."

Dawn raised an eyebrow. "You're saying you didn't mean all those insulting things you said to him?" she asked. "That you liked him?"

"No." Carolyn shook her head and patted her nose with a tissue. "I wish I could say that. But he really was a major league jerk and he did drive me nuts. But I just wanted him to get lost. Not dead." She sniffed loudly, trying to avoid crying again. "I'll be okay." Then she focused on Dawn. "How about you?"

"Depressed," Dawn admitted. "And Shane's even worse. They'd known each other for about ten years. For all his faults, Vince was a good friend to Shane."

"Yeah, he must be really shattered." Carolyn dabbed at her eyes again. "Look, maybe you'd better go home and get some rest yourself. I'll be fine. Mom will look after me." Carolyn managed a weak grin. "Hey, I'll get waited on hand and foot for once. I promise to milk this for all it's worth."

That almost cheered Dawn a little. "What a con

artist," she said, standing up. "Okay. I'll call you in the morning to see if you'll be at school, okay?"

"Sure."

Dawn walked the short distance to her own house and let herself in. Dad was at work, of course, and obviously Mom was, too. Then she realized that she had to call her mother. She'd almost forgotten in all the excitement and stress. It took a little while for them to locate Dr. Jacobs, and she'd been asked if it was important. "Very," she answered. Her mother had picked up a moment later.

"What is it, love? I'm really busy right now." She sounded as stressed out as Dawn felt.

"Did they bring in Vince Holloway?" she asked bluntly and to the point.

"Uh, yes." Mom had to think about that. "He's not a priority, I'm afraid." In a gentler tone, "You do know he's dead?"

"Yes. That's why I'm calling. He had the same dreaming thing that Candy and Jesse had. I thought you should know. There may be tests you can do."

"You're sure?" Mom asked sharply.

"Certain. He was convinced he was being eaten alive by bugs. He freaked before he ran into the road." The memory of the impact made Dawn shudder again. "And remember, he thought he'd been abducted by aliens."

"Right." There was warmth and a little excitement in her voice. "Thanks, sweetheart. I'm going to see if I can get permission for an autopsy. It may help us understand this thing."

"I just hope it helps Candy."

"Me too." Mom hung up.

Dawn sat back on the sofa. After kicking off her sneakers, she slid her feet under her and let out a huge sigh. Maybe there would be something—anything!—to learn from Vince's death that could help her friend. Candy had been in and out of a drug-induced sleep for almost a week now, and her body was getting weaker all the time. Her dreaming hadn't stopped once in all that time. The prognosis wasn't hopeful, but there might just be something that would help.

There had to be!

Fixing herself some herbal tea, Dawn wondered what to do with herself. She wasn't feeling too strong, and it was impossible for her to concentrate. The perfect state for watching a talk show. She flicked on the TV and started watching something about women stealing their best friends' husbands, but she really didn't care what it was. Even the commercials didn't bother her as much as usual.

Dad arrived home just when Dawn was losing all interest. The last two shows had been about makeovers, and Dawn hated those. How come there was never anything the right kind of mindless on TV when you desperately wanted to vegetate? Wasn't TV *supposed* to be junk food for the mind? At least with her dad home, the two of them could make dinner together. She wasn't sure what it was they made and ate, but her lack of attention hadn't ruined it too much. Dad put Mom's share away to reheat later, then Dawn wondered what she was going to do next.

The doorbell rang.

"I'll get it!" she called. To her surprise, Shane was there.

"Uh," he said, rather embarrassed. "I know you said to phone, but I really wanted to talk, uh, if this is a good time?"

She felt better just seeing him. "Of course, come on in." Over her shoulder, she called to her father, "It's Shane!"

Dad hopped out of the kitchen. "Hello," he said, studying him. "You're her Shane? Nice to see you." He frowned. "You're not going on a date or anything tonight, are you?"

"Uh, no," Shane said. "Not today. But I had to talk to Dawn—if it's okay with you, Mr. Jacobs?"

"Of course it is," Dad replied. "Maybe it'd be quieter for you in the den? I'm going to catch the news on TV."

"Okay," Dawn agreed. She led Shane inside and shut the door so they wouldn't hear the TV. Managing a slight smile, she asked, "Is there a reason for the chat, or did you just want to see me?"

"I wanted to see you," he admitted, "but there *is* a reason. I've been doing some thinking." He grinned slightly. "Dangerous, I know. Anyway, maybe it's because I'm still in shock or something, but I've had a few really weird thoughts, and I really need to run them past you. You'll probably tell me I'm cracking up, but I'm willing to take the chance."

Dawn gestured for him to sit beside her on the couch. It was nice to have him so close, even though she wasn't feeling at all romantic. Not with Vince killed earlier, and Candy still hovering between life and death. She wondered if things would ever be good again. "Well," she promised, "I'll try to pay attention. But why me?"

"Because you're the smartest person I know as well as the prettiest." He sounded sincere, not just trying to flatter her. "I'm sure you'll spot all the weaknesses —and help me. And you know Candy Watson best."

"Go on."

Shane took a deep breath and then said, "Jesse and Vince and Candy have got to be connected. It's impossible to consider the idea that all three should coincidentally crack up in very similar ways. They've all done weird stuff, and two of them are dead." He became visibly uncomfortable as he added, "And Candy isn't getting any better."

"That's pretty much what Carolyn and I have been thinking," Dawn admitted. "Vince follows the same sort of pattern—dreaming, sleeplessness, and delusions. But we couldn't make much more of it than that. There's no real connection between them."

"Wrong," said Shane firmly. "They all went to our school. They're all our age and were in our classes. And they were all very bright."

Dawn didn't quite understand. "What do you mean?"

Shane hunched forward. "Look, if you take three people from the school purely randomly, what are the odds that they'll all be the same age and all be in the honors programs? Vince and Jesse were in English honors with us—Candy is in music honors. None of them are athletes, jocks, or even average. What does that suggest to you?"

"Being bright is dangerous to your health?" Dawn suggested less than seriously.

"Yes," he agreed, surprising her. "*Very* dangerous, if not deadly."

"Okay," she said. "I'm telling you right now that you're sounding pretty darned weird to me. What are you getting at?"

"All three of the victims of this whatever-it-is disease are really smart kids," Shane explained. "People with high IQs and vivid imaginations. *Too* vivid. Look, Vince was obsessed with UFOs for as long as I've known him. He believed implicitly that little green men were visiting earth. More than anything he wanted to meet them. And then yesterday he claimed he did on Monday night. Can that be a coincidence? That's when he came down with his sleeplessness and hallucinations."

"And Jesse Stern's big dream was to be a pilot," she added. "He ended up thinking he could fly and fell to his death."

"Click," agreed Shane. "Two people, two dreams—same result. What about Candy?"

"Candy adores attention," Dawn replied. "She loves being noticed. And was she ever noticed when she stripped!"

Shane blushed at the memory. "Three people, three dreams. All of them were convinced that their dreams were *real*. Or, in Candy's case, that reality was just a dream, and it was okay to wander about the school in the buff."

"But Vince was ranting on about bugs," argued Dawn. "That wasn't his greatest dream."

"No, it was his greatest nightmare." Shane shrugged. "He had a phobia about insects. He was talking about his wild dreams when I said that he was bugging me. In his state, that must have been enough to trigger his phobia. He was convinced he was being attacked by insects. The key point is that just one word set him off so that he was utterly terrified and ran into those cars."

Dawn could see the links. "But what could make them all behave in those bizarre ways?" she asked.

"I don't know, exactly," Shane admitted. "But whatever it is, it obviously works by stimulating the brain. Candy's dreams are in overdrive. Vince was really hyper this morning. Jesse was oblivious to the world. This whatever-it-is seems to set people's imaginations racing, until it kills them. That's why it's targeting the honors students—they have the most vivid imaginations."

Dawn shivered. "You make it sound like this 'thing' is intelligent—picking people."

Shane shrugged again. "Maybe it is. Or maybe it's some kind of disease that only works on people with really active imaginations."

"If you ask me," Dawn replied, "*you* have a very active imagination. You'd better be really careful." Struck by what she said, she gasped, "You don't think there will be *more* people affected, do you?"

Grimly Shane nodded. "I'm certain of it. Unless the docs can figure out what's causing this, I think that everybody at school in the honors program is going to have to be considered a potential victim. Me, you, Carolyn, Andrea—any of us could be the next to come down with it."

CHAPTER 10

Dawn was appalled and terrified to think that they were all vulnerable to this mysterious illness. But she realized that Shane was right—as long as the cause remained unknown, then there was a chance of infection. Or whatever it was. Dawn was scared—for herself and for her friends. Two people dead already, and one in terrible condition. Now the rest of the kids had to be considered possible victims. And they still had no idea what was causing it, let alone any way to cure it.

"Are there . . ." She stopped and swallowed hard.

Her voice had come out high and squeaky, and she had to force herself to calm down. "Are there any more links between the three of them?"

"I've not been able to figure any out," Shane replied. "Jesse didn't hang around with Vince. Let's face it, *I'm* just about the only person who could stand Vince for any length of time. And Candy didn't have much to do with either of the guys outside the classroom. And I can't think of anywhere else the three of them might have gone, either alone or together, except for really obvious places like the mall. And too many people go there, so that can't be the source of the problem."

Dawn nodded. A nasty thought slid into her mind. "What about another person in common?" she asked. "Is there anyone that all three of them might have hung around with who could be the cause of this thing?"

Shane shrugged. "Well, there's *me,*" he said. "I hung around with Vince, and I did meet Jesse a couple of times after school. But I didn't really have anything much to do with Candy until after she was infected."

"I didn't mean *you,*" Dawn protested. "I didn't think you were a common factor. What I meant was maybe there's someone who's got the infection—or whatever it is—but is somehow immune to the disease. Kind of like Typhoid Mary, you know? Infects others, but is only a carrier."

"Or," added Shane grimly, "who is *deliberately* infecting people for some reason."

Dawn was shocked. "You think somebody might be

deliberately killing teens?" The idea was unexpected and terrifying.

"It can be a sick world," Shane said honestly. "People do kill other people, sometimes for the stupidest reasons. We can't rule out the idea that this is being done by someone with a grudge or something. Or just sick pleasure in seeing people die. I mean, we've been assuming that this bizarre behavior is brought on by a disease or something. But what if it's some kind of drug or poison? It's possible that there's a person out there who's giving it to kids."

Dawn hated the thought, but Shane was right; they had to consider it. All at once she shook her head. "If there was a drug or a poison, the autopsy on Jesse would have found it. And look at all the tests they've done on Candy without finding anything. If there was a substance used, it would have to be completely unique and virtually undetectable. What are the chances that someone has developed such a substance and then is using it to kill off smart kids? It doesn't make any sense."

Shane sighed. "Maybe it does if there's someone who had a grudge against all of them?"

"Who?" asked Dawn. "Vince was a pain at times, but he was harmless. He may not have had many friends, but he didn't have any real enemies either. Jesse was pretty popular. And Candy—well, she turned a few people off with her grandstanding, but basically she's a really nice person and almost everyone likes her. I can't think of anyone who'd want to harm even one of the three, let alone all of them."

"Me neither." Shane rubbed the back of his neck. "We're really not getting too far, are we? Well, now it's time for me to really put my sanity on the line. I'd been hoping not to have to suggest this, but—"

"But *what?"* Dawn demanded.

"Maybe Vince was right," Shane suggested. "Maybe he *did* see a UFO and *was* abducted."

Dawn raised her eyebrows. "You really think that's possible?"

"Who knows?" Shane spread his arms wide. "The universe is a big place, and there are billions of stars and planets out there. The chances that there aren't other intelligent races out there have got to be almost nonexistent. And if there are aliens, and they can travel between the stars, then surely they'd be interested in the earth?"

"Look, I love science fiction, too," Dawn answered. "And I agree, there *must* be life somewhere on other planets. And I agree that there could be some who've developed space flight and even come to this planet. But"—she held up her hand—"I just can't accept Vince's story. I mean, why would aliens travel all this way, sneak around, let themselves be spotted, but not contacted? And then kidnap people from their beds to run stupid medical tests on them? If these aliens wanted to know what humans were like, why not land openly and talk to people? This alien abduction stuff is just too dumb for me to believe."

Shane nodded but didn't give up. "That's assuming that they think the way we do. If they exist, they're *alien.* Maybe they have a rule against interfering with other cultures—you know, like that noninterference prime directive in *Star Trek.* They aren't allowed to contact us openly, but they're studying us."

Dawn snorted. "I think they could do better than whisking Vince off from his bed to study us," she objected. "And neither Candy nor Jesse ever said anything about flying saucers or aliens."

"Maybe they were scared," Shane suggested. "Let's face it, you think the idea's dumb, and you're pretty open-minded. What do you think the other kids at school would be like? Candy might have been scared of being shunned if she suggested she'd seen a UFO. And Jesse wanted to be a pilot. He might have thought that he'd have problems getting a job if he had a history of seeing UFOs."

Dawn had to admit that he had a point in both cases. "Maybe," she conceded. "But even if we accept that they *might* have seen aliens, where does that leave us?"

Shane shivered. "With the idea that maybe the aliens are causing this dreaming thing. Vince didn't know what else they might have done to him, because he said that he lost consciousness. But he *did* say they injected something into him. And if it's something alien, maybe it's so alien that the doctors can't detect it."

The thought was almost incredible. But Dawn had to consider it, because they didn't have much else. "You mean that these theoretical aliens of yours might *deliberately* be infecting us? But why?"

"I can think of two possible reasons," Shane replied. "First, that they're trying an experiment of some kind. Maybe to boost brain power. Maybe they're telepathic, for example, and can't talk to us. That would explain why the smartest kids are taken. Maybe they're trying to make us telepathic, so we can talk to them. But maybe instead their experiment is overloading people's minds and making them die from dreaming."

Dawn shook her head. "Then why are all three here in Brookville?" she objected. "Why not all over the world? I think there would be something in the papers if kids from all over the world were being infected like this. And, second, how dumb are these aliens that they don't realize the experiment isn't working and that they're killing people instead of helping them?"

"Maybe they're desperate?" Shane suggested. "They *have* to succeed for some reason, and they have no choice but to keep on trying?"

"Maybe," conceded Dawn. "But we're getting way desperate if we go that far. So, what was your other idea for why they're doing this?"

"Maybe they're deliberately killing us."

"What?"

Shane leaned forward, his face troubled. "Maybe they know that they're killing us, and that's what they're after. Maybe they're developing some kind of bacteriological warfare weapon that will kill people, and Jesse, Vince, and Candy were their experimental guinea pigs. Maybe it's some kind of weird way to conquer the world—kill all the people here and just walk in and take it over."

The idea was scary and troubling, but Dawn couldn't bring herself to accept it. "That's just *too* weird," she said. She realized she was trying to convince herself as much as Shane. "An alien invasion of earth, starting here in our little town?"

"It would have to start somewhere," Shane pointed out. "But you are right—at the moment, it really is too way out. But I haven't been able to come up with another explanation that makes even that much sense. This whole thing is just too much for me to understand. But, honestly, we've got to come up with some sort of answer. If we don't, I'm certain that there are going to be more victims of this thing. Maybe you or even I could be next. And that terrifies me, Dawn."

Before Dawn could speak, there was a gentle rap on the door, and her mother entered the room. She looked tired but also a little cheerier.

"Hi, guys," she said. "How are you doing?"

"Coping, I guess," Dawn replied. "It's been rough."

"Any news, Dr. Jacobs?" asked Shane. Dawn realized he was almost desperate for a positive reply.

"A little," Dawn's mother informed them. "There was something in the back of my mind about Jesse Stern's death that didn't come back to me till today. Remember how your friend Vince said he'd been abducted by aliens?"

"Do we ever," Dawn said with a sigh. "We were starting to think that maybe he was telling the truth. That's how desperate we are for an explanation to all this."

"Well, he was telling a part of the truth," her

mother said. Seeing Dawn's surprise, she added, "I don't know about the alien part of it, but the bit about something being implanted in his leg was perfectly true."

"Yeah," agreed Shane. "That cloudy thing on the X ray, right?"

"Right." Dr. Jacobs smiled slightly. "I remembered that Jesse had a little inflammation on his leg, too, and checked back on the reports. Several X rays were taken, since he'd broken four bones when he fell. One of them was in his leg." She paused so her next statement would have greater impact. "Under that area of inflammation, there was a cloudy patch on the X ray. Again, we thought it was just a minor thing, but it was in the exact same place as the one in Vince's leg."

"Wild," muttered Shane, fascinated.

"It gets better," Dawn's mother informed him. "Vince's parents gave permission for us to examine his leg. We managed to isolate the problem site and removed it."

"So what was it?" Dawn almost screamed.

"I'm not sure," Mom replied. "It was like a small bunch of nerve cells. Little tendrils had fastened into Vince's own nervous system, but it definitely wasn't something that grew there. The DNA and everything is all wrong. It was certainly an intrusion into his body."

"An infection?" asked Shane. "Like a disease, you mean?"

"No, not quite. More like a parasite." Dr. Jacobs sat

on the arm of the couch. "You see, a disease is really a virus or a bacteria that gets into the human body and then feeds off the body to breed and spread. This thing—whatever it is—didn't grow. It simply attached itself to Vince's nervous system and stayed there. The logical conclusion is that it somehow sent signals to Vince's brain to make him dream more."

"Then why didn't you detect it earlier?" demanded Dawn. "Didn't it put out chemicals you could have spotted?" She didn't want to accuse, but she didn't understand why it hadn't been found earlier.

"No," her mother answered. "It used Vince's own body to do that. No foreign chemicals, only those produced by Vince's own body. There was nothing in his system that wasn't supposed to be there."

"Except this nerve knot," Shane finished.

"Right." Dr. Jacobs gave a small smile. "Well, when I discovered all of this, I immediately called Dr. Calfa and suggested that he X-ray Candy's leg."

"And he found one of those nerve clusters?" asked Dawn eagerly.

"I knew you'd figure it out," Mom said approvingly. "Yes, she's got one in her thigh, too, in exactly the same spot as Jesse's and Vince's."

"Yes!" exclaimed Shane happily. "So now we have a common link! All three of them have that nerve knot!"

"Right on target," Mom agreed. "The three of them have the same symptoms and the common intruder."

Dawn felt a tremendous sense of relief. Finally, a

glimmer of light! They had at least got an idea of what they were looking for. "So what happens now?"

"Well, there are several possibilities," her mother informed her. "It's always possible that this invader is a by-product of the real cause, but we're fairly certain it is, in fact, the infecting agent."

"Can you give Candy something to kill it then?" Dawn asked hopefully.

"I wish we could," Mom answered. "But it's a cluster of nerves. Anything that would kill it would affect Candy's own nervous system, perhaps fatally."

Dawn felt let down. "So what *can* you do?"

"Dr. Calfa thinks the best solution is to operate." She patted her daughter's hand. "It would be a relatively simple process, and he's certain he can get the main mass out quickly. The smaller tendrils can be lasered. It can be done in about half an hour, tops. He's asked Mr. and Mrs. Watson for permission for the surgery, and if they agree, he'll do it early tomorrow morning."

Dawn gave a heartfelt sigh. "And that should cure her?"

"With any luck, yes."

"Will you let us know how it goes, Dr. Jacobs?" Shane begged. "We're all really worried about her at school."

"Of course," Dawn's mother agreed. "I promise you, I'll call you at school tomorrow just as soon as there's anything to report." She smiled fondly at her daughter. "I know how close you two are." To Shane, she said, "I'm really sorry about Vince. But something good may still come out of it."

"I think he'd have liked that," Shane replied. "Thanks for everything you've done."

"I just wish I could do more," Dr. Jacobs said. "We still haven't discovered the origin of this strange parasite or what it's doing in Candy's body. We must know that."

"Otherwise there'll be further cases, won't there?" Dawn asked. "Shane and I were worrying about that before you came home."

"Yes," her mother admitted. "There will be further cases. But if the surgery tomorrow works, we'll be able to deal with them."

Dawn sighed. "That's assuming we can identify the people who are infected—before they do something dumb that kills themselves."

CHAPTER 11

The following morning Dawn got to Mr. Belding's class early. She tried to focus on reading *A Plague of Pixies,* feeling she should be getting into it for her project, but her mind refused to cooperate. She still couldn't stop thinking about Vince's death and Candy's upcoming surgery. The Watsons had approved the operation, and Dr. Calfa should be starting at nine.

At least now they had some idea of what was happening. But was Shane's crazy theory about aliens being behind the strange deaths correct? The idea that sleepy old Brookville might be the target of an alien invasion was almost too insane to accept. But only almost. There was a nagging doubt.

Would the operation cure Candy? Removing the infection might do the trick—if the nerve knot *was* the cause and not a symptom instead. Only if they did the procedure would they have a definite answer, though. It was impossible for Dawn not to worry about her friend. She was in such fragile shape after all this time that there was a danger of complications even if the operation went well.

Somebody sat beside her. Dawn jumped, not even realizing there was anyone else in the room. She'd been so lost in her thoughts and fears. It was Shane, who gave her hand a squeeze.

"You're cold," he said.

"I'm scared for Candy," she told him. "They're going ahead with the surgery this morning."

"We can only pray it's successful," Shane told her. "Your mother said she'd let us know how it goes."

The others were starting to file in now. Andrea came in and stared at Dawn and Shane with a raised eyebrow. The sarcastic comment Dawn expected didn't come, though. "I'm sorry about Vince," Andrea said.

"Thanks," Shane replied. Andrea nodded and sat down a few rows back. The other kids acted uncomfortable and were unusually quiet.

Dawn wondered how many of them had figured out that any of them might be the next one affected by whatever had resulted in Jesse's and Vince's deaths. Her eyes scanned the room. Would one of them be next? Would Shane? Would she?

Then Mr. Belding came in, and the class began.

It was impossible to concentrate on Shakespeare, and Dawn's eyes kept straying to the clock. Was the operation over yet? Had it begun? Was Candy recovering? Was she—

Don't even *think* about that possibility!

The clock seemed to be frozen. Every minute dragged, and Dawn's nerves were getting more and more frayed. What was happening? Anything? Nothing? She glanced at the clock again. Just after nine. The hand clicked over another minute.

Without warning Mr. Belding abruptly screamed. His book fell from his fingers and clattered to the floor. Crumpling at the knees, the teacher followed it down in a heap.

"Jeez!" exclaimed Shane, jumping to his feet. He dashed to the front of the class, Dawn right behind him.

Mr. Belding was out cold, his face pale, his breathing ragged. "Loosen his tie," Dawn said firmly. Her mother had insisted on her taking first aid classes, and the lessons came back automatically. Shane obeyed, and together they rolled him on his back.

"Can I do anything?" It was Andrea.

"Water," said Dawn firmly. "Then get the nurse, fast." She didn't look to see if Andrea obeyed. Instead, she pressed her fingers to the artery in the teacher's neck. The pulse was strong, but way too fast. His heart must be hammering away like crazy! Still, that meant no need for CPR, and he was breathing okay, even if in short, sharp gasps.

"What's wrong with him?" asked Shane, worried. "You don't think *he's* infected, do you?"

"No," said Dawn. Her mind was racing. "He's fainted for some reason. Like somebody smacked him on the back of the head with a baseball bat. He's had some kind of shock."

"Heart attack?"

"No, his pulse is strong, though it is very fast. But he didn't seem weak or anything."

Shane shrugged. "Maybe overwork." He managed a slight smile. "Or not enough sleep. He *is* a newlywed, you know."

"I don't know," Dawn told him. "Maybe it's just stress." The door opened, and the school nurse and principal came in. Dawn moved aside to let the nurse check out Mr. Belding.

"What happened to him?" asked the principal.

"He just gave a yell and then collapsed," Dawn told her. "I've no idea why, but he seems to be stable now."

"Do we need an ambulance?" the man asked the nurse.

"It would be best," the nurse agreed.

"I'll tell the secretary," Dawn volunteered and took off running all the way to the office. As she was turning to leave, she saw Carolyn arrive breathlessly.

"Any idea where the nurse is?" she gasped. "Mrs. Belding just collapsed."

"*Mrs.* Belding?" echoed Dawn. "You're kidding!"

"About this, no." Carolyn stared at her friend. "Why would I be?"

"The nurse is with *Mr.* Belding," Dawn told her. "*He* just collapsed." A trickle of icy sweat crawled down her spine. This was way too bizarre!

Carolyn looked as stunned as Dawn felt. "Him, too?"

"Yeah. Come on." They headed back to the classroom as fast as they could. The nurse had tucked a sweater under Mr. Belding's head but not moved him from the spot where he'd fallen. "The ambulance is coming," Dawn said. "But Mrs. Belding's in trouble, too."

"Oh, dear," said the principal. "Maybe it was something they ate? Food poisoning?"

"The symptoms are wrong," the nurse answered. She glanced at Dawn. "You seem to know what you're doing," she said. "Stay with him till the medics arrive." Turning to Carolyn, she added, "Let's go."

The principal looked flustered. "Um, the rest of you had better get along to your next class," he said. Then he turned and shot after the nurse and Carolyn.

Dawn saw the shaken expressions on her classmates' faces as they quietly filed out of the room. A moment later only Shane remained with her, his face reflecting his worry, uncertainty, and shock.

"*Both* of them collapsed?" he said slowly. "That's

one of the strangest things I've ever heard. I mean, if they'd passed out at different times, maybe I'd believe it was food poisoning. But—at the same time, almost exactly?" He shook his head as if trying to clear it. "Why are things getting darker, not clearer?"

"You think this is connected to the infection?" Dawn asked.

Shane laughed. It was brittle sounding, not amused, as if he would have preferred to scream instead. "How could it be a coincidence? All three infected people were in classes here. Now two teachers flake out at the same moment." He shook his head, harder this time. "There's *got* to be a connection. If only I could figure out what it is."

Dawn tried to think things through. "Mr. Belding doesn't have the infection as such," she said slowly. "He was acting perfectly normally until he passed out. And the infection makes you unable to sleep. Whatever has happened to him and his wife is not the same as what happened to our friends."

"No," agreed Shane. "But it's connected somehow. It *has* to be."

"I can think of one connection," Dawn offered. "All of this started since the Beldings were married."

Shane suddenly leaned over and gave her a quick kiss. "Not quite!" he said excitedly. "It all happened since they came back from their honeymoon!"

"So what's the difference?" The kiss had been too quick and unexpected, and she wasn't sure what to make of it—except that it was nice.

"Balbec," Shane said. "It's *got* to be." He shook his head. "That name rings a bell somewhere in the dim recesses of my mind. I'm going to have to look it up tonight."

"The town they stayed in?" Dawn said, puzzled. "Where they had that invasion of pixies?"

"Pixies!" Shane said as if he'd never heard the word before. "Dawn, you *are* a genius!"

She flushed at his praise. "Thanks. But *why* am I a genius?"

"Balbec was invaded by pixies in the sixteenth century," he said, obviously piecing it together as he went along. "And we're invaded by aliens in the twentieth." He gripped her shoulders. "Read that book Mr. Belding lent you tonight. *All* of it! I've got a few ideas of my own, but I think we're on to part of the answer at least."

Dawn still couldn't follow what he was getting at. "Okay," she promised. "But what is this all about?"

"Have you ever read Jacques Vallee?" he asked.

Before she could reply, there was a commotion in the hallway, and then two EMT people came in with a stretcher. Dawn and Shane stood aside to let the man and woman get to Mr. Belding. They gave him a quick examination.

"Is he okay?" Dawn asked anxiously.

"Seems to be," the woman said. "We'll take him in for a thorough work-up, though."

The male ambulance worker sighed. "Seems like we're getting an awful lot of work from this school lately." He and the woman loaded Mr. Belding onto a gurney and then wheeled it out of the room. Dawn and Shane followed.

Reaching the main doors, they saw that there were two ambulances outside, lights flashing. A second team had Mrs. Belding on another gurney and were already loading her into their vehicle. There was a small knot of students and teachers watching. As Dawn passed the office, the secretary waved to her.

"Dawn Jacobs?" she called. "Your mother is on the phone for you."

"Oh." Dawn shot into the office and picked it up. "Mom, what's wrong?"

"Nothing's wrong, dear," came her mother's voice. "I just wanted to tell you about Candy. Dr. Calfa operated and removed the nerve cluster from her thigh at nine."

Dawn couldn't believe she'd forgotten all about that! "How's she doing?" she asked, worried sick for her friend.

"She's fallen into a natural sleep," her mother answered. "It looks as if she's stopped dreaming at last and is getting some real rest. Dr. Calfa is very optimistic about her chances."

"That's great, Mom!" Dawn handed the phone back to the secretary and rushed out of the office. Carolyn and Shane were waiting for her. "Candy's okay. They took out the nerve knot and . . ." Her voice faded away as something hit her. She paled and reeled back. Her friends grabbed at her.

"Dawn!" Carolyn exclaimed. "What's wrong? You feeling okay?"

"No," Dawn confessed. "I just realized something." She stared at her friends. "Candy's operation was at nine o'clock—the exact same time the Beldings both collapsed."

CHAPTER 12

If Dawn had been confused before, that evening her brain was on overload. When she closed *A Plague of Pixies,* she placed it on the table in the den and sat staring at nothing, trying to sort out the thoughts whirling in her head. The book was gripping and at the same time infuriating. She had to talk about it to someone, and Shane had promised to come over. Carolyn said she wanted to practice.

Mom had called to tell her that Candy was still sleeping peacefully and that both teachers had recovered and been allowed to leave. Their collapse had probably been because of overwork, and they'd been advised to take it easy for a couple of days.

Dawn didn't dare say anything about the weird timing of their collapse. It might, after all, be coincidental. But she doubted it.

What connection *could* there be between the Beldings and that mass in Candy's leg?

Thankfully, the doorbell rang, breaking through her frustrating thoughts. It was Shane, carrying a couple of books. "Hi, Mr. Jacobs," he called to Dawn's father.

Dawn dragged him into the den and closed the door, so her father couldn't hear them. She brought Shane up to date on the Beldings and Candy. "It doesn't make a lot of sense," she finished. "I still can't believe their collapses and Candy's operation were coincidental, but what else could it be?"

"There's got to be a connection," Shane agreed. "And I'm starting to get a few ideas on the subject. The only trouble is that some of them are *way* out. I'm afraid you'll think I'm a lunatic when I mention them."

Dawn smiled. "Wait till you hear some of *my* thoughts," she told him. "We may be competing for mad-scientist-of-the-year awards." She sighed. "This whole thing is getting weirder every day." She sat down on the couch, and Shane joined her, placing his books on the table beside *A Plague of Pixies*.

He gestured to the book. "So, what did you learn?"

"I'm not sure," she admitted. "It's a really bizarre story and completely unbelievable. But according to the writer, a bishop, several doctors, and the local town administrators checked the rumors out and said that they were authentic."

"Good." He gave her a wide grin. "So, tell!"

Dawn organized her thoughts. "It seems that in the year 1595, this small village of Balbec was suddenly invaded by fairies—or pixies, elves, goblins, whatever you want to call them. About twenty people over the course of several weeks claimed to have seen them or were taken on strange trips to the fairies' homes. It's all crazy stuff, like the side of a hill opening up and there being a city inside, where the fairies would play and dance and sing. That kind of thing. Then, after about five weeks, the whole thing stopped, and everything returned to normal. The local priest contacted his bishop, who came into the village and ran the enquiry that became the basis for this book. The report was filed away and virtually lost for hundreds of years, but the locals kept the stories alive. That's almost all of it. It's just the usual wild, silly nonsense, except for—"

Shane's eyes were sparkling. "Except for the fact that eight people apparently went crazy and died during this same period. And all eight had reported seeing fairies first."

"Yes!" Dawn stared at him. "How did you know that?"

He tapped one of his books. "I looked up Balbec in this encyclopedia," he explained. "I knew I'd heard the name before. It was quite famous for a couple of years. Nowadays, almost nobody remembers it."

"I'm not really surprised," Dawn said. "Let's face it, it's a dumb story. Nobody believes in fairies."

"Not nowadays," Shane agreed. "But back then, *everybody* did. Even scholars and educated people. The Fair Folk were considered to be halfway between human beings and angels. They were supposed to have fantastic powers, and they were known to kidnap people. Especially babies in their beds and to leave changelings in their places. People were quite scared of meeting fairies, you know."

Dawn smiled and recited:

"Up the airy mountain,
Down the rushy glen,
We daren't go a-hunting
For fear of little men;
Wee folk, good folk,
Trooping all together;
Green jacket, red cap,
And white owl's feather!"

"It's a poem by William Allingham," she explained. "I always loved it."

"It's pretty neat," Shane agreed. "I especially like the fact that even though the wee folk are called *good,* the poet admits to being scared of them. Anyway, think for a minute: little people who kidnap someone, take him away, and then return that person or a changeling home again. What does that remind you of?"

It took a second for the question to sink in. "Why,

Vince's story!" Dawn exclaimed. "But he was talking about flying saucers, not fairies!"

"Right. But nowadays people don't believe in fairies. They *do* believe in flying saucers. That's the difference."

"I don't get it," Dawn confessed. "We're talking about entirely different things here. Magical beings living inside hills with strange powers and—"

"And magical beings living on other planets with strange powers," finished Shane. "Haven't you ever watched *E.T.?* What's he but a very ugly fairy?" He picked up one of the books he'd brought with him. "I asked if you'd read any Jacques Vallee earlier. Well, try this one."

Dawn took the book. It was titled *Passport to Magonia,* and printed under it was *On UFOs, Folklore and Parallel Worlds.* She gave Shane a puzzled glance.

"It's really wild stuff," he told her. "Vallee retells a lot of those old stories about fairies and what was called the Secret Commonwealth—all the nonhuman, intelligent races that were supposed to inhabit this world with us. Then he tells stories told by people who claim to have met aliens from flying saucers—the nonhuman, intelligent races that are supposed to inhabit this cosmos with us. And he shows that they are almost identical stories."

Confused, Dawn shook her head. "He thinks that fairies were actually aliens?"

"No. He thinks that stories of both fairies and aliens are attempts to explain the same experience but done in the accepted cultural norms of the day. Back in the Middle Ages, nobody believed there was life on other worlds. Heck, most people didn't even believe that there *were* other worlds. But a lot of the earth was unexplored. The old maps used to have 'Here there be dragons' written in on unexplored parts. *Anything* might share this planet with us. Sailors reported mermaids as often as people report Bigfoot today.

"But today, the earth's been thoroughly explored. There's nowhere for magical beings to hide—here. But there are lots of places up there." He pointed upward. "Other worlds. So stories that were once told about fairies and their magical chariots or witches riding broomsticks have now become flying saucers, UFOs, and aliens from space. They're still kidnapping people, doing weird things to them, and shooting across the sky, only there's a more scientific explanation for it nowadays."

Dawn tried to sum it up. "So he thinks they're just stories and that UFOs are nothing more than modern fairy tales?"

"No, not quite. This is where it gets really interesting, and I think we may be on to something. He suggests that both sorts of story are based on some kind of reality, but that it's a reality so far out of line with our normal lives that when we run into it, there isn't any normal way to describe it. It's too much for the human mind. So, instead, the mind tries to make sense of it. To recast it in a way it *does* understand. In the Middle Ages, it was meeting fairies. Nowadays it's meeting aliens."

The idea was sparking Dawn's mind. "I get it," she

said slowly. "It's a little like dreaming, where random thoughts are tied together by our sleeping minds to make a kind of pattern. That's why such odd things happen in dreams."

Shane gave her a huge grin. "Exactly! Dreams are definitely tied into this, aren't they? Dreams are often our way of making sense of nonsense. Or, in some cases, of things that are very sensible but that we simply can't understand."

"Like now," Dawn said slowly. "Dreams were involved in all our cases."

"Yes. In all cases," Shane agreed, "there was dreaming involved in some way. And I think we're getting a clue to the reason for it from Candy. She and Vince both had the same problem: dreaming but not being able to sleep. Feverish mental activity."

"The cases of the eight deaths in Balbec," Dawn added. "In those, the people were all wild, ranting, and sleepless. Their deaths were supposedly from possession by demons."

"Or, as we'd say nowadays, madness." Shane gave her a triumphant look. "The connection is there."

Dawn was excited by the idea. Then reality hit home. "But *what* connection?" she asked. "People seeing fairies in Balbec and dying. Vince seeing flying saucers here and then dying. I mean, I can see that there's a link through Mr. and Mrs. Belding, but what *is* the link? Do you think that they're *causing* this somehow?"

"They've *got* to be," Shane argued.

Dawn couldn't believe it. "Look, they're the two

nicest teachers in school. Carolyn and everyone in the orchestra adores Mrs. Belding. She's terrific, caring, and funny. And I don't know about you, but I think Mr. Belding is wonderful. I can't believe he'd have anything to do with *anything* that would result in people's deaths."

"Not consciously, no."

Dawn stared at him as what he said sank in. "You mean that they might be involved but not know it?"

"I'm certain of it." Shane patted her hand. "I like Mr. Belding, too, and I agree that he wouldn't hurt a fly. Neither would his wife. They're great teachers. But, then, people infected with terrible diseases don't mean to pass on their germs. It's simply a fact of life. I think that the Beldings are infected."

"But they aren't hallucinating, are they? And *what* are they infected with?"

Shane didn't answer her directly. "Have you ever read anything by Charles Fort?" he asked her. She shook her head. "Well, he was drawn to strange stories—anything inexplicable, like, oh, fish raining down from the sky, that kind of stuff. Anything that modern science claims is impossible but that people still insist happens. Like sighting a monster in Loch Ness. He wrote several books about that stuff that are great fun to read. And he comes to an interesting conclusion: He thinks we're cattle."

"What?" Dawn couldn't follow this at all.

Shane grinned. "I think he was just being provocative when he said it. What he meant was that he didn't think the human race was the most intelligent species on earth. He suggested that there was another species much more advanced than us, and that they kept the human race for their own needs."

"Like *food?"* Dawn gasped.

"Maybe. Or even as pets." Shane gave her a subdued look. "Either way, the point is that people aren't the last word in evolution on earth. And I'm starting to think that maybe Fort was right."

Dawn thought this over for a few minutes. Shane didn't say a word, obviously realizing it would take her some time for these ideas to sink in.

"So," she finally said, "there's some kind of supercreature that feeds on people. It's so far out of our normal experience that human beings can't even understand it. Somehow it triggers dreams that put people's brains into overdrive. Is that it?"

Shane nodded. "I think it feeds off mental energy. That's why it stimulates the brain. It eats brain waves, if you like, just as we eat french fries. It makes people dream while they're awake and feeds off those dreams. That's why it picks only the brightest kids. They have the most active imaginations—like Vince had. And it's so bizarre that its very appearance starts the whole process. People try to make some sense out of what they see when it appears. Vince saw it as little gray men from outer space. The people in Balbec saw it as fairies. There's no telling what Candy or Jesse saw it as. But whatever it is, it triggers dreams and then feeds off them."

Taking a deep breath, Dawn said, "Even if I can

accept all this—and I don't think I can, yet—there are still two questions that come to mind."

"Shoot."

"First of all, what's the connection between this thing and the Beldings?"

Shane chewed at his lower lip for a moment. "More folklore, I'm afraid. Haven't you ever heard about those old stories of possession? Where a person's mind and body are invaded by demons or ghosts, or whatever? I suspect that the predator we're talking about doesn't have a body, and it needs somewhere to stay."

"Like *inside* the Beldings?" Dawn asked, appalled at the thought. "And they probably don't even know it's there!" She shivered. "Have you ever seen one of those diagrams of the food chain? You know, that start with lots of fish and then lead upward like a pyramid to people? Human beings are at the top of the food chain. But if you're right, we're *not*. There's this thing out there that's above us. And, like the fish, we don't even know there's something ahead of us on the chain."

"That's a good analogy," Shane said approvingly. "This thing feeds on people."

"But why the Beldings?" she asked him.

He tapped *A Plague of Pixies*. "When did this happen?" he asked.

"1595," she answered. Then she caught his meaning. "Exactly four hundred years ago! But what significance does that have?"

Shane pointed to the encyclopedia he'd referred t(
earlier. "According to that book, there was a nev
priest sent to Balbec that year. He was from a villag
in Switzerland. In 1195—four hundred years earlie
—*that* village had been invaded by trolls. A dozen o
so people died of madness."

Dawn struggled to understand. "So you think tha
this predator only has to eat every four hundred years
That maybe it rests between?"

"Yes. I think it woke up this summer while th
Beldings were on their honeymoon in Balbec. Tha
it—or they; there might be more than one predator, o
course—slipped inside the Beldings. When they wen
home, it came with them. Now it's hungry, and it'
started to feed. In a while, it'll be full and fall aslee
again for another four hundred years, when the whol
cycle will start up again. Somebody will visi
Brookville and then leave again with an extra travele
inside him."

It was crazy, but it did make sense of some of th
strange events. "And those nerve knots," she sug
gested, "are something this creature puts into people
A sort of radio transmitter or even a kind of fishhook
It has something to do with the way it feeds on them
tied into their nervous systems."

He nodded. "Hey, that's a really great suggestion
I'll bet that's *exactly* what it is."

Dawn gave a heavy sigh. "It's all so—" Sh
shrugged. "I've got to be really psycho to even thin
that all this makes sense, but it does. And that leave
my second question."

"Which is?"

"How do we stop this thing from killing more people?"

Shane wriggled uncomfortably. "That's exactly what I've been wondering. If there *is* some kind of predator that's much more advanced than we are and hides inside people and kills other people—then how can we possibly stop it?"

CHAPTER 13

Carolyn flexed her aching fingers as she prepared for bed. Her practice had been long and hard, but she was happy. Her technique was definitely improving, and she was really *feeling* the shape of the Vivaldi concerto she'd worked on. She was still humming it softly to herself as she undressed and slid between the sheets on her bed.

She had had a good practice. She had let the music flow through her. And other painful thoughts had been driven from her mind as she concentrated on the music.

Now, however, those other thoughts came crowding back. The thread of the tune she'd been humming was gone, and she couldn't drag it back again. While she had the music, the other thoughts stayed away. But with the music gone, her fears, worry, and guilt came flooding back.

Candy was still in the hospital. The doctors, for all their talk, still knew nothing about her condition. They couldn't be sure if she'd recover because they still didn't know what had happened to her. Carolyn desperately wanted Candy to get better, but there was no way to know if she would.

And Candy was the lucky one.

Carolyn didn't like thinking about Vince, but there was no way she could avoid it. She kept seeing his face when she closed her eyes. Her feelings about him were very confused. She was sad and hurt that he was dead. He had been, well, not a friend, exactly—an acquaintance. A pest, really. She hated his attention when he had been alive and suspected that Dawn thought she'd just been playing hard to get. But that wasn't the case—she had really hated Vince's incredibly dumb attempts to get her to go out with him.

He'd been so creepy, wrapped up in all that parapsychology and UFOs and other weird stuff. She didn't understand any of it, and he was so intense about it. Carolyn felt it was dangerous to mess with that kind of material. Even if there was nothing to it, it did major damage to your head. It had certainly made Vince really wacko.

And for another thing, Carolyn was too involved

with her music to be interested in dating anyone. It would distract her, split her attention, and she couldn't afford that. Carolyn was determined to be a great violinist. Her heroine was Ofra Harnoy, the Canadian cellist, who had made her Carnegie Hall debut when she was just Carolyn's age. And you only got to be that great by practice and by living the music. A guy might be fun, but he'd be a distraction, and Carolyn didn't want anything to distract her.

But . . .

Somewhere in her mix of emotions, she felt a strong dose of guilt. There was the small voice inside that wouldn't stop harassing her. *If you'd been nicer to Vince,* the voice whispered, *maybe you could have saved his life.*

It was nonsense. It had to be. It wasn't her fault that Vince had died. It wasn't anybody's, really. It had been this bizarre sickness. The same one that had killed Jesse Stern. The same one that Candy might or might not recover from. There was nothing that she, Carolyn, could possibly have done to help Vince. It had been completely out of her control.

It *had!*

Eventually, troubled, she fell asleep.

Carolyn's eyes opened suddenly, and she stared out into the grayness of her room. In the dim light from her window, she could make out the vague shapes of her furniture and the clothes she'd draped across her chair when she'd gone to bed. Nothing there, nothing to bother her. She must have been having a bad dream, that was all. It must have woken her up.

Wriggling, she scratched at an itch on her arm before trying to settle back to sleep. Her throat felt dry, however, so she sat up to get herself a glass of water from the carafe she kept beside her bed. As she started to reach for it, she froze in sudden terror.

There was a vague glow on her closed bedroom door. A light from outside, maybe, shining through the window? No, the small pool of light from the window fell onto the carpet, not the door. The light was dull, greenish, and glowing, like phosphorescence. She didn't know why, but it scared her. She couldn't tear her eyes away as she watched the tiny threads of light. They were moving, weaving in and out, like glowing worms.

Then she realized that it was getting larger. It had started as a spot and was now the size of a baseball. And still it grew, writhing and pulsing with that sickly greenish glow.

What could it be?

Carolyn wanted to scream, to call out, to wake her parents. She didn't want to be alone with whatever this was. She wanted to throw back the covers, to leap out of bed and run. She couldn't do anything but sit and watch, a faint whimpering in her throat the only sound she could force out.

The twisting light was now the size of a basketball and still growing. It was as if something were moving up a long tunnel toward her room or like a balloon being inflated. She was shaking with fear, the taste of bile in her mouth. She didn't know what it was, but she knew this brightness was *wrong.*

Then it seemed to explode, the sickly green glow flooding her room now. With a startled cry, Carolyn covered her eyes to shield them. Peeking out between her fingers, she saw that within the light was a figure. She couldn't make out anything except the outline, but it was someone walking toward her.

Then the glow died down, and she could lower her arm and see clearly.

She wanted to faint.

In the sickly glow, Vince stood and glared at her. He was the same disgusting color, except his eyes, which burned red. His face was twisted with anger, and he hunched forward slightly.

Carolyn whimpered again, fear gripping her and making her shake. Her skin was icy cold, and she could feel the hairs on her neck stand up. She tried to look away but couldn't.

"Carolyn!" Vince cried loudly. His voice was raw with anger and pain that echoed in the small space.

"Go away!" she gasped. "Go away! You're dead!"

"Yes," he agreed, his voice hissing, his eyes sparking with fury. "Yes, I'm dead—and it's all your fault."

"No," she insisted. "No! It wasn't my fault! There was nothing I could do!"

"Nothing?" Vince laughed—an ugly, sneering sound. "Nothing? You could have given me something to live for. Instead, you rejected me. And now I'm dead!"

"It wasn't because of me!" Carolyn said. "It was because of that disease."

"Oh, sure," drawled the ghost, contempt and loathing in his voice. "Find something else to blame. Of *course* it wasn't your fault. You did nothing to feel guilty about, did you? Just humiliated me daily, trashed me to my friends, and then publicly rejected me. And I loved you so much, Carolyn. You were the light of my life. When that light went out, there was no reason left for me to live. *That's* why I died. It was *your* fault!"

"No!" she sobbed. "You're twisting everything. That's not what happened! It isn't! I didn't do anything!"

Vince jerked forward, so that he was only two feet from her now. Even though she was terrified, Carolyn was alert enough to notice that she could see through the ghost and the light in the room was shining out from within Vince.

"So now I'm a liar as well as a fool?" Vince snarled. "Have you no pity for me at all? Nothing in your twisted, vicious little heart but hatred for someone who only wanted to love you?"

"Stop it!" begged Carolyn. "Please, Vince, leave me alone! It wasn't my fault. I'm sorry you're dead, but it wasn't my fault!"

"I'll leave you alone," Vince told her, taking another step forward, his transparent, ghastly green face only inches away now. "But there's a price for you to pay. You rejected me when I was alive, and you've got to pay for that."

Carolyn felt nauseated but was still unable to look away from his terrible face. "What?" she gasped. "What are you talking about?"

His blazing red eyes stared into Carolyn's, peering all the way into the depths of her soul. "You have to make it up to me," he said softly, the anger and hurt still seething in his voice. "You have to give me in death what you wouldn't give me in life. I want your love, Carolyn."

"You're insane!" she told him hysterically. "I can't just decide to love you like that! I can't help it, Vince! I can't love you!"

The ghost howled with dreadful rage. Vince threw his arms high and screamed, "Still she seeks to hurt me! Even after she's killed me, she won't let me rest!"

"Vince," Carolyn pleaded, sobbing, "you don't know what you're saying. You've got to leave me alone. You have to stay away from me! Leave me alone, please!"

He whipped his face down to stare into her tear-filled eyes again. "I'll leave you alone, you tramp," he snarled. "But not until I've gotten something out of you first." His fist came up—it, too, green and transparent. Then Vince darted his hand forward to grab a fistful of her short hair. Carolyn yelled as his ghostly fingers held on painfully. Laughing, he yanked back on her hair, forcing her to look up at him. Then he bent down, his face within inches of hers.

Carolyn whimpered as his spectral lips met hers. She gagged, wanting to throw up, but he wouldn't let her go. He lingered over the kiss, and she couldn't move, couldn't fight back. She was held in his terrible grip.

And then he did release her, throwing her down on the bed. "One more thing," he told her mockingly. He gripped the sheet that covered her and tore it aside. His eyes burned again, as if he could see through not just her nightie, but also through her skin and bones below. She felt unclean and degraded as well as disgusted and terrified. Those burning, dead eyes seemed to take in every inch of her body. Her skin crawled beneath that blazing gaze. "A body to die for," he sneered. "And I *did* die for it. Well, if you're going to live, then you'll bear my mark!" He reached out toward her thigh.

Carolyn froze. What was he going to do? Tear off the skimpy protection of her nightie? How far did this manic ghost aim to go in his obsessive love for her? Was Vince satisfied with that kiss, or did he want more from her?

She was almost relieved when his hand didn't touch her nightclothes. Instead, the fingers brushed her naked thigh. It was an icy touch at first, then Vince gave a cry of rage and *thrust* his fingers into her leg, penetrating the muscle. A consuming pain shot out from that spot, enveloping Carolyn completely.

Her nerves overloaded, and shocked, Carolyn blacked out.

When she awoke the next morning, there was natural light streaming into her room, and she could hear the birds singing outside. A tremendous wave of relief washed over her.

It had been nothing more than a bad dream. That was all. She'd been feeling a bit guilty over how she'd treated poor Vince while he was alive, and that guilt had produced the dream of his angry ghost. Nothing had really happened, no matter how vivid her memory of the dream might be. She could almost feel those ghastly lips kissing hers and see those blazing red eyes. She could almost feel the—

No! She *could* feel the place where he had jabbed her with his hand. There was a dull pain in her thigh. She sat up, shaking slightly, afraid of what she would see.

There, about six inches above her knee, was a red, swollen spot on her skin that hadn't been there the night before.

The mark that Candy had. The mark that Vince had, right before he died.

The mark that meant madness and death—now on her . . .

CHAPTER 14

Sick and trembling, Carolyn simply stared at her leg. She was infected. She was going to go insane. Then she would die. She wanted to scream, to throw up, to—

She had to call Dawn! Dawn's mother might be able to do something for her! She had talked about that operation on Candy. Maybe they could do that now and save her life, too!

Carolyn tried to jump out of bed. As she did so, her leg gave way beneath her. With a cry, she fell to the carpet and lay there for a moment, sobbing. There had been such pain in her leg when she tried to stand on it.

She rolled onto her back and saw that the redness was worse. It was going to kill her.

Gradually, though, the throbbing died down. Carefully, she attempted to stand. This time she made it. Her thigh felt sore, but the pain was diminishing. Maybe that mark *wasn't* the infection? Was it possible that it was just an insect bite or even a rough spot she'd scratched? She had a vague memory of scratching her arm the night before. Had she scratched her leg, too, and caused this red spot?

No. She was just trying to evade the issue, she knew. There couldn't be any doubt. She'd been infected, and she was doomed if nothing were done about it. She crossed to her bedroom door, favoring the injured leg. After slipping on her robe, she headed down the stairs to the kitchen. She'd use the phone there to call Dawn and—

And *what?*

Carolyn stopped, several steps from the bottom of the stairs, puzzled. She was going to call Dawn and—something. But what? Why did she want to call Dawn? She'd sec her in an hour or so at school. There wasn't anything desperately urgent that couldn't wait till then. Carolyn shrugged and went back upstairs. She'd have a quick shower, then get dressed. She had time for a bite of breakfast before the bus came.

As she sprinted back upstairs, she started to hum the Vivaldi melody from the previous evening.

Life was fun.

* * *

Dawn had spent a very sleepless night, and it showed. She looked like hell, she knew, as she walked slowly into the school. There were probably bags under her eyes, and she should have washed her hair. But how could she sleep if what she and Shane were thinking was correct? That there was some kind of monster hidden within the two best teachers in the school, waiting to prey on their brightest students?

And neither she nor Shane could think of anything to do about it.

The trouble was, their theory was just *so* far out that she didn't dare talk to anyone or ask for advice. She could imagine where that would get her! "We think there's some creature lurking in the depths of Mr. Belding's brain that hops out at night for a quick snack off his students' imaginations and dreams . . ." Despite her somber mood, the thought did bring a smile briefly to her face.

She'd be locked up for observation at the hospital. The *mental* hospital.

Dawn wished she could believe their theory *was* crazy. The main problem was, it was the only one that fit all of the facts. The minor problem was that there was simply no way to actually *prove* the theory. Her mind was a mess right now, with all her fears, worries, and disturbed thoughts. That brought another smile to her lips. The state her brain was in right now, she was probably safe from the creature. It would get severe indigestion trying to eat her dreams!

There had to be something they could do to fight

this thing, though. Dawn had read enough fantasy stories to know that fairies were supposed to be afraid of iron and that salt was effective against a host of nocturnal monsters. Holy water, crucifixes, and garlic dealt with vampires.

But what could you use against a monster without a body that lurked in the recesses of people's minds?

The frustrating thing was that she was convinced there *was* an answer. There had to be. Otherwise, there would be millions of these mind-dwelling monsters about, feeding like crazy. They were long-lived, so they *must* have been detected before and somehow dealt with. Dawn had decided to try the local library for information, but she knew it wouldn't be possible to ask a down-to-earth librarian for help in discovering a way to kill nonmaterial monsters.

Unless she pretended it was for a story she was writing . . .

That might work. The idea made her feel a little cheerier. Spotting Carolyn helped lift her spirits, too. Her friend waved and joined her as they walked into the school building. "How did your practice go last night?" Dawn asked.

"Terrific," Carolyn replied. "You know, I really think I'm getting there. It feels so good to hear the music flowing." She grinned. "How was your evening? Did Shane come over? Did you get in some serious lip action?"

"Don't I wish," said Dawn with a sigh. "We spent the whole time just talking about this weird infection and what we could do about it."

Carolyn pretended to gag. "What? Well, I hope it was a real good discussion."

"I'm not sure that's exactly how I'd describe it." Dawn shrugged. "I don't know what we achieved aside from scaring me so badly I could hardly sleep."

"So that's why you look so lousy," Carolyn commented.

"Oh, thanks. Like I *really* needed to hear that!"

"Sorry, but if I don't tell you, others will." Carolyn put an arm around Dawn's shoulders. "What *did* you come up with?"

Dawn shook her head. "It's too complicated to tell you right now," she replied and decided not to go to the library after school. She needed to talk to her friend first. "Can you come over after school? It's really freaky, and you've got to take in a lot of stuff. Otherwise you'll just think I've lost what few marbles I had left." She sighed. "Heck, even *I* think I'm probably crazy."

"After school?" Carolyn shrugged. "Sure. No problem." Then she frowned. "You know, I'm sure there was something I wanted to tell you, but I can't remember what."

"If it's important," Dawn commented, "then it'll come back to you."

"Right," agreed Carolyn. "Whatever it was, it can't be life or death, can it?"

Dawn was surprised and disappointed not to see Shane. She wondered if he was playing hooky to do some research or whether there was some other reason for his not being in school. When she was in Mr.

Belding's class, she couldn't feel comfortable. She surprised herself by taking a seat next to Andrea. It must have surprised Andrea, but she didn't comment. Dawn couldn't stand the thought of a whole period with the English teacher without someone beside her.

She avoided looking in Mr. Belding's direction as much as possible and found herself wondering what it must be like for him. If she and Shane were right, there was something utterly inhuman living inside the teacher, hiding in his mind, watching the students to pick out its next meal.

Dawn shivered.

"You okay?" Andrea asked quietly. "You look like you're trembling. Do you think you're coming down with something?"

Terminal fear, thought Dawn. "I'm okay," she whispered back. "Just a chill, I guess." A chill right through to her bones . . .

Eventually, though, school was over. She sat next to Carolyn on the bus home, hunched over, lost in her thoughts. Carolyn caught on and didn't interrupt. She was humming snatches of music, her eyes sparkling. Dawn was glad that her friend was obviously doing so well with her music. She knew how much it meant to Carolyn.

No one was home when the two girls reached the Jacobses'. Mom was obviously at the hospital, and Dad had a sales conference, so he would probably be late. At least that left her and Carolyn free to talk without the fear of being overheard. Dawn didn't want to imagine what her parents would think of her wild theory. There was leftover lasagna in the fridge, so Dawn microwaved some for her and Carolyn. She wouldn't tell Carolyn anything about her theory until they'd eaten. She figured it was going to take a lot to convince Carolyn that there was anything to believe in.

Plus, she knew, she was delaying deliberately. Carolyn was bound to think she was nuts. But if she couldn't convince Carolyn, Dawn knew she'd never be able to convince anyone.

The doorbell rang. Dawn wondered who it could be—maybe an overnight delivery for her father? To her surprise and pleasure, it was Shane.

"Hi," he greeted her. "Can I come in?" He had another bundle of books with him. "I've been heavily into research today."

"Hey," called Carolyn from the kitchen doorway, "am I intruding here? Maybe I should leave the two of you alone?"

"No," Dawn said with a little reluctance. "Actually, I'm glad you're here, Shane. I was just going to tell Carolyn what we discussed last night."

"Well, I hope she's got a real open mind," Shane quipped.

"So open," Carolyn assured him, "that many people think my brains fell out the gap." She shrugged. "So, what's this secret theory of yours?"

They settled down at the kitchen table. Dawn poured both of her guests sodas to drink as they talked.

"We don't think that Jesse and Vince died because

of a disease exactly," Dawn explained. "Or that it's a disease that Candy is suffering from. We think it's a kind of parasite."

Carolyn shrugged. "So? Bugs either way, right?"

"Not quite," Shane said. "We think that there's a kind of intelligence behind this. That it isn't exactly a virus or something that is passed on. We think there's a creature that's feeding off people's imaginations. That it provokes sleeplessness and dreaming to help it feed from its victims' minds. And that the so-called mass or nerve knot in the leg is, well, something like a radio transmitter, sending out mental energy waves to the feeding creature." He grimaced. "So I guess you think we've both cracked up, right?"

"No." Carolyn smiled. "It's a bit crazy, I'll grant you, but you must have something other than your fevered imaginations to back this up, I assume?" She hummed a couple of bars of Vivaldi, then stopped. "Sorry, I keep getting unfocused, don't I? Why don't you fill me in on the details of this theory?"

Dawn did so, helped by Shane. Together, they sketched out the problems of Balbec and the way it had been infested. They told her about the Vallee theories and Charles Fort and the mysterious connection between the Beldings and the illnesses. When they were finished, Dawn wondered if they had been convincing or just plain confusing.

Carolyn shook her head, humming her tune again. "It's weird," she finally announced. "But it does seem to fit a few of the facts." She smiled at them. "And you two are too intelligent to be completely suckered by a dumb idea."

"And it explains the weird dreams, too," Dawn said, glad that her friend was on their side. "It's the way the human mind tries to make sense of the unknowable."

"Speaking of wild dreams," Carolyn offered. "I had a real winner last night. I guess Vince's death affected me more than I thought, because I could almost swear his ghost came back to haunt me last night."

Dawn didn't know what to say. She gave Shane's hand a quick, comforting squeeze when she saw the pain that crossed his face. "Maybe you're wishing you'd been nicer to him," she said to Carolyn.

"I guess." Carolyn sighed. "On the other hand, he was acting pretty nastily in the dream—accusing me of killing him. He even attacked me." She shuddered. "Not at all like the real Vince. That's why I'm sure it was just a dream. But it was really vivid." She started to hum her tune again.

Dawn was hit in the pit of her stomach. "Carolyn," she said, surprised at how high and thin her voice came out. "How real did it seem to be?"

Her friend stopped humming and shrugged. "As real as this does. But it couldn't have been."

Dawn glanced at Shane. He'd gone white. Terrified of the answer she'd get, Dawn turned back to Carolyn. "Did he try to hurt you?"

"Yeah." She snorted. "Not like Vince, is it?"

Dawn stood up very slowly. She was scared she'd

faint if she moved any faster. Carolyn was wearing a long skirt and a blouse. "Pull your skirt up," she ordered.

Raising an eyebrow, Carolyn gave a nervous laugh. "Are you sure that's quite proper?" she asked.

"Do it," Dawn ordered. "If you don't, I will."

Carolyn got to her feet. "Dawn, what's with you?" she asked, worried. "Are you feeling okay? Why this sudden fascination with my legs?"

"Because I think you've been infected," she said, the icy fear in her heart making her voice cold and faint. "I think that's what happened to you last night. Not a dream and not a ghost."

"Trust me," Carolyn said, sounding a little worried herself. "I'd know if anything had happened to me. I'm fine." She started humming again as she rose and backed away from the table.

Shane leaped to his feet and grabbed Carolyn's arms, pinning her against the cabinets. Carolyn gave a startled cry and tried to break free. "Stay still!" Shane snapped. To Dawn he said, "Take a look. Quick."

Dawn yanked up the hem of Carolyn's skirt to midthigh. Her throat went dry as she saw the bright red welt on her friend's leg.

"It's there," she gasped, the fear building inside her. "She *is* infected." She stared at Carolyn in horror. "We have to get you to hospital, right away."

"I'm fine," Carolyn insisted. "There's nothing wrong with me. Nothing at all." She started humming again.

"Nothing?" echoed Shane. "You've got to be kidding. Carolyn, if you're not treated, you'll be *dead* soon."

"Nonsense," Carolyn insisted between notes.

That was one sign of the infection, Dawn knew. The parasite was feeding off her dreams and thoughts. Because Carolyn adored music, her response was to sing or hum or play. It was the start of the feeding cycle that would end with Carolyn dead—unless they got help for her. "I'll call Mom," Dawn told Shane. "You make sure she doesn't get away."

"Right," he agreed. He loosened his grip slightly but kept hold of Carolyn. She didn't seem to be aware that she was being held. She was humming happily to herself.

Dawn crossed to the phone. Her best friend was now infected, just as Candy was. She couldn't even start to sort out how she felt. To have both of her friends in this state! It was dreadful. Still, there was at least a way to deal with it. She dialed the hospital and asked to be put through to her mother.

"I'm sorry," the receptionist replied. "She left here a short while ago. I believe she was on her way home."

"Thanks," Dawn said, hanging up the phone. She turned to Shane. "She's on her way home and could be here any time."

"That's good," Shane answered. "That way she can check Carolyn for herself. But I'm certain she's been infected."

"I know." Dawn felt sick. "But Mom will remove that thing from her leg. Then she'll be fine, won't she?"

"I'm sure she will." Shane gave her an encouraging smile. "Listen, isn't that a car now?"

"Yeah!" Dawn ran to the door and saw with relief that her mother was climbing out of her car. She ran outside, incredibly glad to see her mother. "Mom! It's Carolyn! She's infected, too! You've got to get her to the hospital and remove that tumor from her leg!"

Dr. Jacobs sighed heavily. "I don't think I can, sweetheart," she said. There was pain and tiredness in her voice, and she looked absolutely beat. "Are you sure about Carolyn?"

"Come and see." Dawn was getting scared again. What did her mother mean? Grabbing her mom's arm, she virtually dragged her into the kitchen. Pulling up Carolyn's skirt, she showed her mother the mark.

Dr. Jacobs probed it gently with her fingers. "Yes," she agreed. "It's just like the others. You're right—Carolyn is infected."

"But," said Shane hopefully, "she'll be okay, won't she? You can take the thing out, like you did with Candy, can't you?"

"No." Dawn's mother sighed again. "Look, I came home early to tell you. Candy's dead."

CHAPTER 15

"Dead?" Dawn echoed in a strangled cry. She felt as if she were about to faint. "She can't be!"

"I'm sorry," her mother said softly, hugging her close. Dawn wasn't sure who was supposed to be comforting whom. "She died just a couple hours ago. I wanted to tell you in person, not over the phone. I know how close you were."

"But she was getting better!" cried Dawn, anger and loss blazing through her words. "You said so! She was sleeping!"

"I know," Mom replied. "But she simply slipped away. She was sleeping but never woke up again. She drifted out."

"No," whispered Dawn. She knew that Carolyn was as good as dead as well. Tears trickled down her cheeks in burning streams.

"So, you see," her mother continued softly, "I can't possibly agree to Carolyn's tumor being removed. The same thing might happen to her as happened to Candy."

"But—but she's going to *die!*" wailed Dawn. She glanced at her friend through tear-fogged eyes. Shane was still holding Carolyn tightly, but Carolyn seemed to be completely oblivious to everything. She was wearing a silly smile and humming away to herself. She was getting worse by the minute, just as the others had. She was slowly being cut off from reality. The end result would be madness and death. And there didn't seem to be *anything* that anyone could do to prevent it!

"Not if I can help it," her mother promised.

Dawn wished she could believe that. But she knew her mom was just being supportive. What *could* she do? There had been four known victims of this killer now—and three of them were already dead. What chance did Carolyn have of surviving? Dawn gave a sob at the thought of losing Carolyn as well.

Would this never end?

Refusing to give in completely to the mounting loss and fear, Dawn struggled free from her mother's hug. "We'd better get her to the hospital anyway," she said, fighting back her tears and distress. "At least the doctors can keep an eye on her."

"Definitely," Mom agreed. "Bring her out to the car."

Shane finally spoke, the first time since Dr. Jacobs had broken the news. "What are the chances for Carolyn?" he asked. There was definite worry in his voice. "Really?"

"Really?" Dr. Jacobs shook her head. "I wish I could tell you we can save her, but I can't lie like that to either of you. But I will say that the only way she stands a chance is if we discover what's causing this in people." She fished the car keys from her bag and started for the door.

The bemused girl didn't offer any resistance as they got her into the backseat of the car and sat on either side of her. Carolyn hummed away happily to herself, totally lost in her dream world.

How long did she have left?

Dawn wasn't sure whether her mother would listen to their wild theory, but she had to try. It was Carolyn's only chance. "Remember the other day?" she asked as her mother started the car. "When Mr. and Mrs. Belding both collapsed at school?"

"Sure," agreed Dr. Jacobs, backing down the driveway into the road. She was concentrating on her driving, not looking at Dawn.

"They *both* collapsed the exact same moment that the tumor was taken out of Candy's leg." It was hard to mention Candy's name without crying.

"That's odd." Her mother was focused on the road

as she sped through the twilight streets. "But can't this wait?"

"It's more than odd, Dr. Jacobs," Shane said. "It's significant." He gave Dawn an encouraging smile. "We think it's connected."

"Connected?" Dawn's mother was puzzled. "But how *could* it be connected?"

"Well," Dawn said, "we have a very odd theory. But maybe we'd better save it for later."

"A good idea," her mother agreed. "Let me concentrate on driving. When Carolyn's checked in, then we can talk."

After Carolyn had been admitted to the hospital and her parents notified, Dr. Calfa called down to check on her. Dr. Jacobs took Dawn and Shane to the staff lounge. Dawn was feeling very shaky, both physically and emotionally, and she was glad for the chance to sit down. Her nerves were badly frayed, and she knew it wouldn't take much to make her either scream, cry, or go crazy. Shane appeared to be holding up a little better—or else he was simply hiding his emotions.

"Now," Dawn's mother said, pouring herself a cup of strong coffee, "let's hear this wild theory of yours. What possible connection could there be between Candy and those two teachers?"

For the second time in one day, Dawn had to expound the theory she and Shane had evolved. It sounded even weaker to her this time around, and she was certain that all she would succeed in doing would be to convince her mother that she'd cracked under the strain. Despite this, she plunged on with the tale, with Shane breaking in from time to time to add his own observations and to amplify some of the evidence.

When Dawn finished, her mother threw out the paper cup she'd been using. "So," she said, "let's see if I've got this straight. You both think that there's some kind of parasitic creature living inside the Beldings that only ventures out at night. It then attacks people, planting those nerve clusters in their thighs. Somehow it increases the mental processes of its victims, forcing them constantly to use their imaginations. Then eventually it drains their mental energies, resulting in their deaths. Is that about it?"

"Yes," Dawn agreed, a sinking feeling in her stomach. Put so bluntly, it *did* sound pretty stupid.

"Then it should be fairly easy to check," Dr. Jacobs commented.

Dawn couldn't believe that her mother hadn't simply laughed in their faces. Her amazement must have shown on her face, because her mother smiled.

"I don't mean that I believe in this theory," she admitted. "But your theory does have the virtue of being able to explain what nobody else can. And you've done it scientifically, which means that we have a number of ways to check it out."

Dawn winced. "But are you trying to prove or disprove our theory?" she asked.

"Does it matter?" her mother argued. "If you're wrong, then we should be able to convince you. If you're right, you should be able to convince me."

"In other words," Shane said carefully, "you think we're wrong."

"Yes," Dr. Jacobs admitted. "But that doesn't mean that you *are* wrong. I have enough respect for your brains to admit that you may be smarter than I am."

Dawn sighed. Still, it was probably the best they could have expected. At least Mom hadn't dismissed them or wanted them to check into a good mental hospital! "So," she asked, "how do we go about getting proof one way or the other?"

Her mother smiled slightly. "The Beldings were both brought here when they collapsed. I can access their files on the computer and check their records. If there really is something nonhuman inside them, it must have left a trace. Odd readings, abnormal responses, that sort of thing. It may be very subtle, of course, and take a lot of hunting."

It wasn't.

Dawn could hardly believe their good fortune when her mother got on the computer and found the traces on the first attempt.

"That," her mother said very slowly, "is *definitely* bizarre."

There was an electrocardiogram in each file. And both tracings showed what appeared to be two heartbeats. Dr. Jacobs skipped to the notes, shook her head, and gazed back at Dawn and Shane. "The technician comments that there must have been something wrong with the machine. It was taken off-line and recalibrated. Before the Beldings could be tested again, they'd recovered and checked themselves out."

Shane tapped the wavy line on the screen. "*Two* heartbeats each?" he asked. Dawn could understand the awe and uncertainty in his voice. Despite her own conviction that they were on the right track, she hadn't been expecting anything like this.

"Maybe," her mother said. "Of course, the technician may be correct, and there was some sort of glitch."

"Do you really believe that?" Dawn asked, disappointment clear in her voice.

Her mother snorted. "That two people who collapsed at the same instant as the surgery on Candy just happened to be tested by a broken machine? Come on, Dawn—give me credit for *some* brains, please. Well, they can't possibly both have two hearts, and the same machine couldn't give wrong readings on both of them. There's got to be something here, all right."

Shane stared at the screen. "Why do I feel like we're watching that scene in *Alien* where that little nasty thing bursts out of the guy's chest?" he asked.

Dawn shivered. "I don't think it's really like that," she said. There was more hope than certainty in her voice, though.

"It may not be a double heartbeat anyway," Dr. Jacobs added. "The EKG machine registers the electrical activity associated with the heart. If you're right and this parasite inside them is only semimaterial, then it has to be electrical in nature. We could be reading its traces in this scan. It wouldn't have a heart as such, because it wouldn't be completely material."

"So," Dawn said, "this is proof, right? We can *prove* that the Beldings are infected, can't we?"

"No," her mother answered, seeing the pain and frustration on Dawn's face. Gently she added, "All this does is raise possibilities. We need to get the Beldings in for further tests. Maybe a CAT scan would show us whatever this parasite is. But it would have to be voluntary, and the Beldings didn't seem keen to hang around here for follow-up tests."

"Doesn't that mean that they *know* something would show up?" Shane asked eagerly.

"No," Dr. Jacobs argued. "It just means they don't like medical checkups. A lot of people don't like tests, you know."

"And, besides," added Dawn, "this parasite may not be able to control their minds exactly, but it has to have *some* measure of control over them. It managed to convince Carolyn that she wasn't affected even though she was. It probably has convinced the Beldings that they're fine and don't need tests."

"That's my girl," her mother said affectionately. "I'm afraid you're probably correct. *If* this parasite exists, it's got to have some way of protecting itself. Unless the teachers agree to come in for tests, we can't do much." She waved at the graphs. "Those things may convince you, and they may make me wonder—but that's all."

"Mom," Dawn said desperately, "Candy's *dead,*

ınd now Carolyn's infected. That parasite is *killing* ny friends. There's got to be *something* we can do."

Her mother shook her head. "Maybe there is, but I lon't know what. Look, it's late, we're all tired and ınder stress. I think that we have to just pack it in for onight. Carolyn is staying here for observation. If we ;an get a good night's sleep, we may be able to ıpproach this fresh tomorrow."

Dawn didn't want to stop, but she realized that her nother was right. She checked her watch. "Ten-ifteen!" she exclaimed. "I didn't realize it was so ate."

"A lot's happened," Shane told her. "If you could lrop me off on the way home, I'd be really grateful."

"No problem," Dawn's mother agreed. "Let's go."

Dawn prepared for bed slowly, every muscle in her ›ody aching. Her eyes were red rimmed from crying, ınd her emotions were barely under control. This had o have been the worst day of her life. Candy was lead, leaving a terrible, ice-cold void. Candy, the iveliest, most cheerful person she'd ever known—it vas so hard to realize she'd never see her again.

And now Carolyn was infected. She was already ıallucinating, her mind teetering on the brink of nadness, her body gearing up for death. It was ıorrible to have lost Candy, but if Carolyn was the ıext to die, Dawn couldn't imagine how she'd be able o go on herself.

If only there was some way to fight back! But even if hey could somehow prove that there was this bizarre creature that fed on mental energy, where would it get them? Neither she nor Shane had come up with any ideas of how to stop it. How could they if it could simply invade a person's body.

It reminded her of something. Invading people's bodies . . .

She slipped between the sheets, trying to focus on that thought. Then it came to her—those days in Sunday school as a child, hearing the stories of devils and demons who could slip inside unwary people and possess their bodies and souls. Were those stories perhaps based on experiences like this one?

Various ideas started to coalesce in her mind. The old stories about witches, who had the mark of the devil on their bodies. Could that have been like the strange masses on the thighs of the victims? The idea that animals could be taken over by the demons, too. And that they could be destroyed by holy water, exorcism, and sunlight.

Was it time to call in the exorcist? She almost managed a smile at that thought. But would that be the best way to go? To try to find someone who might be willing to perform an exorcism on the Beldings?

She couldn't imagine that the teachers would allow it to be done. Mr. Belding hated anything that even touched on superstition, and exorcism was not exactly considered authentic even by churchgoers. Besides which, how would she go about finding an exorcist? She doubted that there'd be a listing in the Yellow Pages.

But she was certain that she was on the right track

now. She had been certain that over the centuries *some* people must have discovered the existence of these parasites. Okay, there was a lot of superstition mixed in with the facts, but maybe there were answers in Shane's and Vince's books. It was worth checking at the very least.

After all, Carolyn's life depended on her discovering a solution.

CHAPTER 16

Dawn suddenly sat up in her bed, her heart beating wildly. For a moment she was disoriented, her bedroom seeming foreign and alien to her. She was confused, uncertain what had woken her up. She glanced at the night table, frowning.

The clock was there, but she couldn't read it. It somehow appeared to be less solid than it should have been. In fact, so did the table itself. As she glanced around her room, everything was in that same odd state. It was as if she were looking at a faded photo:

everything was there but washed out. She had a feeling that if she stared at anything long enough, she'd be able to see right through it, like Superman with his X-ray vision.

Dawn chuckled at the thought. Weird things had happened lately but not *that* weird! The idea that she'd somehow developed see-through vision was a little too bizarre. She stared down at the covers on her bed and almost jumped.

She *could* see through them, too, as if they were transparent. She could see her nightgown right through the sheets. It was light green, off the shoulder, and fell halfway down her thighs. She got out of bed, the sheets extraordinarily light as she threw them off. Standing on the carpet, she felt quite comfortable, despite her flimsy gown. It was a warm night.

The room became even less real as she walked to the window. Her vanity and chair were there, but she could see the wallpaper *through* them. She put out her hand and touched the back of the chair. It wasn't solid, it felt jelly-like instead of wooden. She touched the top of the vanity. She could have simply pushed her hand through it if she wanted. She reached for one of her hairbrushes and managed to grip it, but it was like holding on to smoke. When she tried to pick the brush up, it slipped through her fingers.

This was wild! With a laugh, Dawn spun around and almost danced to the window. As she approached the walls, they seemed to fade even farther away. It was as if they were made of smoky glass, and she could see the grass of the back lawn through the supposedly solid wall! The window might as well have not been there at all.

Despite the fact that it had to be the middle of the night, it was light outside. Not from a street lamp or porch light, but as if day had begun early. It was like a spring morning, with soft light everywhere. Without really thinking of what she was doing, Dawn simply moved forward.

Through the wall. It was like walking through tissue paper—a moment of resistance, and then she was outside. She laughed again in delight and looked back at her room. The wall was intact (she'd half expected a Dawn-shaped hole!) and she could still see right through it.

There was a faint breeze that stirred the hem of her nightie, but she felt warm enough. Dawn wasn't really thinking about what she was doing. This was obviously just a dream, and it didn't matter what happened. She started to walk across the lawn, staring around her with pleasure. It was like a magical morning, and she was utterly at peace.

Their backyard was actually quite sizable—almost two acres, in fact. Beyond the lawn was an area that her parents had simply left wild. From time to time, they would see chipmunks, rabbits, or a groundhog. There was a family of raccoons living out there somewhere. They all loved watching the wildlife, and Dawn was a little disappointed that there weren't any animals out foraging right then. She suspected she'd be able to walk right up to the shyest of creatures in her current state without scaring them off.

Then she stopped at the edge of the trees, puzzled. There was a bright glowing light among the trees. Her first thought was that there was a fire burning. But there was no smoke nor the sound of wood crackling and burning. For another, the light was a soft golden color, not the angry red of flames. So what could it be?

Only one way to find out! Dawn started into the trees. She could vaguely feel sticks and stones under her bare feet, but they were just like everything else—much too unreal to hurt. She wasn't even getting dirty walking barefoot.

As she drew closer, Dawn saw that the light was coming from what looked like a hole in the side of a small hill. Now that she thought about it, she didn't recall any such hill in their yard! But it was there now and quite real. She moved toward the hole and stopped, astonished.

It was as if there were a doorway cut into the ground. It was about seven feet long and three feet wide. Beyond the opening was a passageway that glowed with golden light.

This was definitely beyond bizarre now! Not at all frightened, Dawn stepped into the doorway. There was a vague smell of earth and humus about her, a sort of rich, gardeny scent. The passageway seemed to extend thirty or forty feet ahead of her, sloping down slightly into the ground.

"My lady, welcome."

Dawn gave a start as she realized that there was someone in the tunnel with her. She couldn't make out anyone at first. She heard a movement, and then the speaker came into focus. She stared at him in awe.

He was about her height and very slender. His face was thin, the cheekbones prominent. His ears were slightly pointed, his hair was a dusty golden, and his eyes were a pale blue. He was both ghostly and yet very real. Tearing her gaze from his gentle, pleasant face, she saw that he wore some kind of trousers and tunic, both made of a pale green material. He had on leather knee-length boots and a long cloak that almost reached to the ground.

"My lady," he repeated, "you are indeed most welcome here."

"Here?" Dawn asked. "In this hole in the ground?"

The stranger laughed. "Ah, but this is no mere hole, my lady," he answered, his voice very musical. "As I am sure you are well aware."

The only thing that Dawn was well aware of right then was that she was standing talking to one of the most handsome men she'd ever seen, and she was wearing nothing but a thin nightie! She couldn't stop blushing. "Maybe I'd better leave," she said, not wanting to go. "I'm not really dressed for company."

The man laughed again. "You look delightful," he told her and held out a hand. "But you are quite correct. That robe is not meant for travel." He eyed her critically. Dawn didn't feel that he was looking at her naked flesh, but that he was sorting through possibilities. Then he muttered a few odd-sounding words and waved his hand.

The nightie was gone, replaced by real clothing. Dawn gasped as she looked down to see that she had on a long dress made of some rich, green velvety material, trimmed with gold. On her feet were slippers of a similar material. It was lovely, and Dawn couldn't resist twirling about happily. The dress felt comfortable and very expensive.

"I trust that I have chosen an acceptable dress?" the man asked.

"It's marvelous," she assured him. "But how did you do that? I mean, just make it appear like that?"

He gave her a puzzled look. "It is something that all of the Fair Folk can do, my lady. As you are to be our guest this night for our festivities, I wished you to be attired in a fitting manner."

The Fair Folk! Dawn gasped. She was a big fan of fantasy stories, and many of them had characters based on the Fair Folk, or fairies, as they were often called. That strange, nonhuman race that shared the earth with people once but who retreated underground when humans crowded them out.

And *she* was to be their guest for a night!

Excitedly, Dawn followed her guide down the passageway. "What's your name?" she asked him.

"I am Tristram," he replied.

"My name's Dawn," she offered.

He smiled back at her. "Naturally," he agreed. He gestured at her red hair. "Such color could only be a gift of the rising sun."

"Flatterer." But Dawn felt oddly pleased with his compliment. They came to the end of the passageway, and Dawn could see the source of the golden light clearly now.

Ahead of them was a huge cavern. Dawn felt certain that there was no way they had come down far enough under the ground to make this place possible, but she suspected that it followed its own laws of reality. The cavern had to be a mile across in all directions and several hundred feet high. Almost filling the space was a—well, was it a building or a city? Or a bit of both?

It was incredible, that was for sure! It appeared to be constructed out of soaring, impossibly thin towers and light, airy arches spanning the towers. It was like Cinderella's castle at Disney World, only a thousand times larger and more complex as well as being made from stone that glowed gold. Spires, domes, and turrets adorned the building/city, and flags and banners fluttered in the gentle breeze. Doorways and windows dotted the walls and towers, and Dawn could see tall, elegant people moving about.

This was the home of the Fair Folk then. She giggled at the thought that the Jacobs family apparently had a whole town of fairies living in their backyard. It was certainly a lot more exotic than raccoons and groundhogs!

She could hear the excited and happy cries of the inhabitants calling to one another, and there was a faint sound of music from within the place. The most delightful of scents wafted around her as she followed Tristram toward the nearest entrance. Flowers bloomed everywhere, despite the lack of sunshine. She supposed that the golden glow of the town itself was more than enough light for any plant.

Tristram took her through the closest doorway, and she was inside the building. The ceiling was high and arched, and everything was built from golden bricks. All about them were more of the Fair Folk—tall, handsome men and dignified, beautiful women. Despite their number, they all looked curiously alike. They were either blond or silver haired. They all appeared to be in their early twenties, she guessed. There were no signs of children or old people. Their eyes were all pale colors, like Tristram's watery blue or else pale brown. Everyone appeared to be in perfect health—nobody had even the slightest sign of acne, and no one was the least bit overweight.

Most of the people nodded or bowed slightly as they passed, but none stopped to talk to her or Tristram. The men wore clothing much like his, and the women wore dresses and slippers similar to Dawn's. The main differences were in the colors. Blues, reds, golds, and greens dominated with a few browns thrown in. White and black were conspicuously absent. It was a riot of color everywhere. Draperies hung from the walls, and the various items of furniture that they passed were of oak or cherry wood. There were, Dawn noted, no mirrors and no sign of anything made of metal.

Tristram led her down a corridor. The sound of music grew louder, and she realized that the smells of food were also getting stronger. The sound of laughter and conversation was on the rise, too. Dawn realized she was being taken to some kind of banquet or party. Hadn't Tristram said something about her being their guest? Was this in her honor then? Dawn felt terribly flattered.

They passed through a final doorway and into a huge feasting room. There were several long tables along the sides of the room. Almost every place was filled, the seats taken by more of the beautiful Fair Folk. The center of the room was clear, and Tristram led Dawn across the space to the table at the far end of the hall. Dawn took a quick glance over her shoulder and saw that there was a small orchestra in a balcony playing the gentle, belllike music that provided the background to the murmuring voices.

It was definitely a feast! The tables were laden with dishes and plates filled with all kinds of foods. Just the smell of it madc Dawn's stomach start screaming for attention. There were roasted meats, cooked birds that must have been ostriches from the size of them, pies, and loaves of twisted breads. There were bowls filled with rice and others with steaming vegetables. Serving people were hurrying about bringing more food and refilling wooden goblets with a bright, golden liquid. Dawn couldn't quite make out the waiters and waitresses. If she looked directly at them, they became nothing more than shadows. But if she saw them from the corner of her eye they appeared to be solid enough, just undefined. It was odd, but she decided she had other things to look at than the servants.

They had reached the main table now. Only three

people were seated there, though there were five empty chairs. They were more like thrones actually—huge, tall-backed seats with armrests and cushions. What appeared to be coats of arms were carved into the backs of the thrones. Dawn noticed this in a second, before her eyes riveted on the three people already seated.

"Your majesties," Tristram said, bowing low, "may I present our visitor, Dawn? My lady, these are King Oberon, Queen Titania, and the Lady Ariane."

Dawn knew her legends well enough to recognize the first two names. Everyone from Shakespeare on had used the names of Oberon and Titania as the king and queen of the fairies. Ariane was a new name to her, but that meant very little. Clearly, then, she was in the presence of royalty. She made a low, graceful curtsey, thankful she knew how!

"You are welcome at our table, Lady Dawn," said Oberon. His voice was heavier and more sonorous than the other men's, though he appeared to be just as young. But there was a weight of authority in his pale eyes.

"Indeed," agreed Titania. "Please, join us here at our modest table." She was, if possible, more beautiful than the other ladies, and she held herself like royalty with great inner dignity. Dawn would have killed to look like that!

Ariane said nothing. Her eyes met Dawn's briefly before she looked away. But in that second, Dawn saw anger and hostility blazing in their dark depths. Dawn had no idea why that should be, but there was no time to worry about it now. Tristram took her hand gently and led her to the seat beside Titania. Dawn couldn't believe that she was sitting with fairy royalty! Tristram then took his own seat beside her. Oberon was next to his wife, and Ariane, on the far side of the king, so Dawn didn't have to look at her again. She felt better knowing that. There was obviously something wrong with the woman.

There was a flicker of movement beside Dawn as one of the shadowy servants arrived to pour some of the golden liquid into her goblet. With another blur of movement, another filled Tristram's. Her guide raised his cup.

"To the fairest lady in the room," he said as a toast, his eyes locked on hers.

Dawn burned with embarrassment and pleasure. "You've got to be joking," she managed to reply. "Everybody here is much more gorgeous than I am."

"Ah, but you have an exotic beauty," he countered, a smile on his lips as he sipped his drink. "You are very different from the pale beauty of the Fair Folk."

Dawn giggled. "You're a real smooth talker, aren't you?" She tried some of the liquid. It was warm and fruity but not too sweet. It was bubbly and absolutely delicious.

"He has a smooth tongue," said Ariane unexpectedly. "And a fickle heart. Last night it was I he was romancing."

"The lady is our guest, Ariane," said Oberon with steel in his voice. "This is her night. You will undoubtedly have the attention you crave again after she has returned to her home."

"Attention, yes," agreed Ariane. "But all the time knowing that it is she he is thinking of."

Uh-oh. Dawn suddenly realized what was going on here. Tristram was obviously Ariane's boyfriend, and she thought that he was paying too much attention to Dawn. "Uh, I'm sure he's only being polite to me," Dawn said.

"I would sooner hear *him* say that," Ariane answered coldly.

"Enough," Titania said. Her eyes blazed at the woman. "This is neither the time nor the place for your spoiled temper. Let Tristram and the Lady Dawn enjoy their time together."

Ariane glowered past the monarchs but settled back in her throne. Dawn knew she was obeying the order, but that it was done with ill grace. Still, she wasn't going to let one woman with an attitude spoil this magical evening for her!

She didn't know where to begin—everything looked and smelled so incredibly delicious. She didn't know how everyone could stay so slim. She'd go crazy and pig out if she lived here! She helped herself to a slice of what looked like steak. Tristram ripped a large chunk from one of the steaming loaves and passed it to her. She accepted it gratefully. It was fresh baked, and the crust snapped as she bit into the soft yeasty middle.

Once again, Dawn noticed that there was no metal

present. The Fair Folk were supposed to be deathly allergic to iron, she knew. The plates were all made of polished wood as were the spoons and forks. The knives were wooden with blades of crystal. She discovered that they cut even the thick steak with ease. The meat almost melted in her mouth, it was so tender.

It was all so marvelous—the people, the setting, the food and drink, the music in the background. It felt as if it had all been taken from the pages of one of her favorite fantasy books. . . .

And then she knew.

With a cry, she jumped to her feet, her heart pounding as she stared about the great hall.

"My lady!" Tristram exclaimed, concern on his handsome face. "Is something amiss?"

"Everything is amiss!" Dawn yelled, backing away from the table. The Fair Folk were staring at her, some in puzzlement, some in concern. Only Ariane had a mocking smile on her face. "This whole thing is a sham, isn't it? It's *you.* You're out there. That predator of dreams. You've come for me, haven't you?"

CHAPTER 17

Oberon turned to Tristram. "Our guest appears disturbed," he commented.

"Disturbed?" Dawn yelled. "You think *this* is disturbed? Wait till I really get going. Then you'll see disturbed!" She glared around the room wildly. "Where are you? Show yourself, you coward!"

Ariane laughed. "And to think you preferred that creature to *me,*" she scoffed to Tristram. "She is clearly insane."

Tristram took a step forward. "Milady," he begged. "Please, calm yourself. I do not know what you mean, but if there is something worrying you, allow me to—"

"No!" Dawn cried. "I won't allow you to do anything. Keep away from me, you disgusting thing." She darted forward, snatching up one of the knives. "Maybe this is just a part of the dream you're forcing me to have," she warned him, "but maybe it can really hurt you. Want to find out?"

Titania slowly rose to her feet. "This human child is in need of help," she said sympathetically. "I had thought that she would have accepted us and understood us."

Dawn gave a wild laugh. "Oh, I understand you, all right! You're forcing me to have this dream to stimulate my imagination, giving me the appearance of what I desire the most to lull me into accepting it as real so you can infect me, just like you infected the others. That's what's *really* happening here, isn't it? There's no hall, no feast, no music, and no stupid dress!" She grabbed a handful of the green velvet she wore and tore at it, anger giving her strength. It ripped free, and she was wearing only her nightie again. "This is what's real, isn't it?"

Tristram was almost in tears. "The appearance of that dress was merely to make you feel comfortable," he explained. "So you would not be embarrassed to be here without clothing."

"I'll bet," snapped Dawn. "It was to put me at ease, wasn't it, so you could get me, too. It isn't working! Come on, you pathetic little monster, stop this stupid charade now and show yourself to me! Face me as you are—if you dare!"

"I think," Oberon said coldly, "that it would be best if you were to take your guest home, Tristram. She is disrupting our festivities."

"As you wish, my liege," agreed Tristram. He took a step toward Dawn, his hand reaching out for hers.

Terrified, Dawn stabbed out with the knife. It sliced into Tristram's hand almost effortlessly. He screamed and drew back, showering blood onto the stone floor.

Ariane laughed, almost nastily. "Poor Tristram," she said mockingly. "Has your little friend hurt you?"

Tristram was gasping, holding his injured hand, trying to staunch the flow of blood. He appeared to be almost in shock. For the first time Dawn started to wonder if she was wrong. She had been so certain that this was an attack by the parasite, but seeing Tristram so pale and shaken, she started to doubt her suspicions just slightly.

And Ariane pounced.

The fairy woman leaped across the back of the chair, almost flying across the space between her and Dawn. Dawn tried to turn, but she wasn't quick enough. Ariane landed on her back and grabbed Dawn's wrists. With a cry, Dawn fell heavily to the floor.

The whole room seemed to dissolve around her. She suddenly felt cold, a chill that penetrated deep into her mind as well as her body. She was back in her own room, on her bed, gasping and shaken. She was facedown, the weight of *something*—Ariane? whatever?—pressed into her back.

Floating in the air in front of her was a yellowish cloud, thin, wispy, and disgusting. Tendrils writhed in the air, and one of these was cut off.

Dawn realized with shock that that was what she had believed to be Tristram. It *was* the parasite. She had been correct. The thing had tried to infect her, but she'd managed to fight it off.

Then what was on her back? She struggled but couldn't move. The weight pressed down upon her, and she gasped and tried to cry out for help. There was pressure on her throat, choking her. As she struggled to free herself, she saw that there was a film of yellowish smoke around her wrists. Then she understood.

There were *two* of the parasites, not one! "Tristram" had been the main one, but there was a second, who had posed as Ariane! It was as if the shutters had been opened on the windows of her mind. She began to understand what these things were. Maybe this mental contact that they instigated was two-way if their victim was awake! She realized that there must always be pairs of these parasites, which was why *two* teachers had to be chosen.

And she knew that they were breeding. That was why they had woken. They were absorbing the mental energy that they needed so that they could have offspring. Then the first two parasites would die, their lives over.

But first they would do the equivalent of laying eggs.

Then, in four hundred years, those new parasites would emerge and find victims of their own, and the cycle would begin again. Unless they could be stopped . . .

But Dawn couldn't stop anything. She couldn't even get free, no matter how hard she fought. Gradually the parasite was winning. Dawn found herself being turned over, no matter how hard she fought. She was getting dizzy from the lack of air, thanks to the clawlike grip the creature had on her throat. She tried to resist, but she was on the verge of blacking out. Panic and terror were willing the last vestiges of her mind as she was forced over and onto her back.

For one moment she was staring up at the parasite as it held her down. Tendrils extending from this second sickly cloud were wrapped about her wrists and ankles and a thicker one about her throat, choking the consciousness from her. The smokiness writhed in pleasure and anticipation, barely inches from her body. Dawn was almost glad she couldn't breath, because she was certain that this thing must have the stench of death about it.

Then a fresh tendril formed slowly. It looked a little like the edge of a knife as it slowly took shape over her. Dawn had no strength left to fight as the wispiness rose and then plunged down, stabbing into her thigh.

There was a second of absolutely unendurable pain, and then she lost consciousness completely.

When she woke, Dawn felt terrible. She discovered that she was upside down on top of the covers in her bed. Her wrists and ankles hurt, and her breathing was raspy. She felt sick, ready to throw up. For a moment she was disoriented and didn't know what had happened.

Then the memory of it came flooding back to her. With a gasp of fear and disgust, she managed to sit up.

There were red welts about both wrists and ankles where the second parasite had gripped her, and there was probably another around her neck. Hardly daring to look, she hesitantly pulled up the hem of her nightie.

On her right thigh was a swollen red mark.

She'd been infected.

Panic filled her for a few moments, and she huddled up, terrified and shaking. She'd been infected and was going to go insane and then die. Just like Jesse and Vince and Candy. And just like Carolyn was doing. She was another victim and—

NO!

She forced herself to stop shaking and fought down the emotional floods of terror. She didn't dare give in to them. She had to fight back, to stop this thing somehow. And she wasn't alone. Shane was on her side, and Mom was almost willing to believe. Together, they'd be able to do something.

And she was certain that the creatures existed. Though the dream about going into the realm of the Fair Folk had been one of the parasites' wish-fulfillment hallucinations designed to start her imagination going into overdrive so they could feed, she was certain that the vision she'd had of the two floating, disgusting clouds had been quite real. That was what these things really looked like when their dreams were stripped away. Bilious clouds of toxic gases, writhing and infecting people.

And she understood why they could only come out at night. Sunlight was filled with energy, which things like solar panels could collect and turn into power and heat. Those cloud parasites had to be vulnerable to powerful light. If they absorbed too much energy, they'd heat and expand and die. They needed somewhere to hide from the sunlight during the day—like inside the Beldings. Then, at night, while their hosts slept, the creatures would emerge to feed.

Dawn was convinced that she was on the right track. It just needed a little more thinking through. The parasites were vulnerable during the day if she could just figure out some way to get at them.

She slowly forced herself to calm down. The creatures had only been able to win so far because nobody knew that they existed. Now, however, they had been exposed. That meant there had to be a way to beat them.

Before she and Carolyn were their next victims.

She started to get out of bed, but pain stabbed through her right leg. That evil nerve knot! It was growing inside her and feeding off her mind, transmitting her dreams and hopes and fears back to those two disgusting creatures. Feeling horribly unclean and contaminated, Dawn managed to stand on her second attempt and staggered into the bathroom. She took a scalding hot shower, trying to wash away the memory of those sickly tendrils wrapped about her. When she was finished, almost all her body was red from the heat. She returned to her bedroom and dressed slowly in a long-sleeved and high-necked blouse that covered the welts on her wrists and neck. She wore a floor-length skirt to hide her ankles and then tied her hair back loosely.

When she noticed that her father was still in bed, she realized it was Saturday morning. No school! One less problem to worry about. Her mother had left for an early start at the hospital. Probably to try to work out a method to save Carolyn, Dawn realized. Her mom was one of the best and wouldn't give in while there was the slightest chance. Dawn grabbed an orange juice and a waffle, which helped to settle her stomach. She looked up Shane's number in the phone book and dialed. A woman answered, and Dawn asked to speak to Shane. A moment later she heard him on the line.

"Shane," she told him, "they got me last night."

"Oh, God." There was a pause and then he said, "I'm really sorry, Dawn. You've got the mark?"

"Yes."

"Well, we've got to—" He broke off and then said, *"They?"*

"I saw them," she told him. "There are two of them, Shane, and they're getting ready to breed. We've *got* to stop them—not just to save Carolyn and myself, but before there are dozens more of these creatures. They really do create incredibly realistic hallucinations, but I managed to break free. I realized what was happening. I guess that's why I haven't forgotten what they did to me, like all their other victims. And there was—I don't know, something like communication between us."

"You *talked* to them?" Shane asked incredulously.

"No, not talk," Dawn admitted. "I don't think that they're intelligent exactly. It's like they steal intelligence from us. But there's some kind of mind there, like that of a hungry, vicious animal. And I could sense things in those minds. I know that they're most vulnerable in the daytime. That's when we have to get them—while they're resting inside their hosts. They're capable of being killed then. What we have to do—"

"What we have to do," he told her firmly, "is to get you into hospital for safekeeping. You could start losing it at any time." There was the unspoken thought that he was starting to wonder if she had *already* begun hallucinating and that what she was so convinced was true was just her imagination going wild.

"No!" Dawn snapped. "Shane, if I'm put into the hospital, then I'll be powerless. I'll just stay there till I die! You and I are the only ones who *know* what's happening. It's up to us to act!"

"Dawn," he answered, and she could hear the agony in his voice, "we can't let you do anything. You're infected. *Anything* that you think from now on could be nothing more than hallucination. You could hurt yourself or someone else and not even know it. Let me talk to your mother, please."

"She's gone to work," Dawn said. She felt hurt and betrayed. "Shane, don't do this to me! Don't let them lock me up!"

"Dawn, it's for your own good," he replied.

With a strangled cry of rage and fear, she slammed the phone down. Shane was going to get her committed, like she was insane! And she wasn't! There was nothing wrong with her—yet. But if she were locked up, she might as well just curl up and die. She couldn't let them take her. She had to act and act fast. Shane was bound to head over here to try to talk to her, so she didn't dare remain. Maybe he thought he'd be doing the best thing for her, but she knew he was wrong. She had to get out of there!

With a smile, she moved quietly through the house to the den. She didn't care what Shane thought—she wasn't crazy. But she would be if they found her. She would be if they locked her away.

There was no way she'd let that happen. She'd act first.

She'd finish off those dream-thieving parasites!

CHAPTER 18

When Dawn hung up, Shane didn't know what to do. She was obviously in a bad state, and he could certainly empathize with that. But at the same time, she seemed to be behaving in a very uncharacteristic way. He couldn't help thinking that she was already under the influence of the mind parasite in which they'd both come to believe.

What was she likely to do next? If it were anyone else, Shane wouldn't have been so worried. On the other hand, Dawn was *very* imaginative and somewhat unpredictable. Whatever she decided to do, it was going to be instant and drastic. His best course of action was to try to stop her and reason with her.

As he was about to leave his house, he realized that backup might be needed. He wasn't absolutely certain that he could stop Dawn alone. Hating to delay, he nevertheless dialed the number for the hospital and asked to speak to Dr. Jacobs.

"She's in the ER right now," the receptionist informed him.

"I know that!" Shane had to restrain himself from yelling. "Tell her this *is* an emergency. It's her daughter."

"Please hold on." It seemed to take forever, but it couldn't have been much more than a couple of minutes before he heard Dawn's mother.

"Hello? Shane? What's wrong?"

"It's Dawn," he told her. "She's been infected as well. I think she's going wild already."

"Oh, God." There was a short pause, then Dr. Jacobs said, "I'm coming straight home. I'll meet you there."

"Right," Shane agreed, but the line was already dead. He hung up the receiver, then shot out of his house as fast as he could. Dawn lived only a half-dozen blocks away. Maybe he'd be in time to catch her.

He wasn't. When he reached the Jacobses' house, he rang the bell. After a moment he rang it again longer. He was about to try a third time when the door whipped open and Dawn's father glared out at him

Mr. Jacobs wore a dressing gown and an irate expression.

"What do you want?" he yelled.

Shane didn't care. "Where's Dawn?" he asked urgently.

Mr. Jacobs glowered at him. "It's Saturday morning," he complained. "I was trying to get some rest. Can't you see my daughter at school?"

Shane shook his head. "This is important. She's in trouble. I've got to see her!" he pushed past Mr. Jacobs. "Dawn!" he yelled, hoping she was still around.

Her father gave him a bemused look. "What's this all about?" he asked. "She isn't here, you know. I'm not sure where she is. I was asleep until you started with the bell."

Shane was starting to panic now. Where could Dawn have gone? "She's sick," he told her father. "I called her mother, and she's coming home. But we've got to find her! We've got to!"

Mr. Jacobs obviously didn't understand what was happening, but he did get the message that Dawn was in trouble. "I'll get some trousers on," he said grimly. "Wait here."

Shane didn't like the thought of standing around while Dawn was doing—what? But he didn't have much choice in the matter. "Okay," he agreed. "Just hurry, please."

"You got it." Mr. Jacobs took off for his room.

Hopping from one foot to the other, Shane waited impatiently. Where was Dawn? Was she in danger?

Was she hallucinating, maybe already doing something that could result in her death? Once the weird dreams set in, he knew, she could do almost anything without thought of the consequences. He had to find her. He had to!

A car drove up the driveway. Shane rushed to the door as Dr. Jacobs hurried up the front walk.

"Is she here?" Dawn's mother asked anxiously.

"No," Shane answered. "We don't know where she is."

"Tell me everything," Dr. Jacobs instructed him. She was clearly forcing herself not to panic. Shane obeyed, relating what Dawn had said when she'd called. Dr. Jacobs looked very grim when he finished. "She obviously feels that she doesn't have much time," she commented.

"She's probably right," Shane agreed, his stomach wrenching at the thought of Dawn infected and dying.

"I agree." Dr. Jacobs scowled. "So—where would she go?"

At that moment Mr. Jacobs reemerged, buttoning his shirt cuffs. "And why did she take my gun?" he demanded.

"Gun?" Shane asked, startled.

"I travel a lot," Mr. Jacobs said. "Some places you're better off with a gun. It makes you feel safer. I was getting dressed and saw that the drawer where I keep it was open, and it was gone."

Shane had a sinking feeling. "Does Dawn know how to use it?"

"Of course she does," her father replied. "I insisted

that she take a course in firearms safety if I was keeping a gun in the house. I wouldn't want her to hurt herself with it."

"Then I think I know where she is," Shane said. He felt sick. "And why she took the gun. She's gone to see the Beldings." He stared into Dr. Jacobs's shocked eyes. "She's decided to end this once and for all. She told me that the parasites are vulnerable in the day. I think she's gone to kill the Beldings."

"Kill?" echoed Mr. Jacobs, aghast. "My daughter wouldn't hurt anyone."

"Not normally," agreed Shane. "But she's hallucinating. She doesn't know what she's doing. She could kill them both without knowing what she's doing."

Dr. Jacobs nodded once. "You're right, Shane." She headed for the phone. "I've got to warn them."

"Warn them?" her husband asked. "Shouldn't we call the police?"

Shane shook his head. "The state she's in, sir, they might have to shoot her to stop her. I think we'd be better off trying to stop her ourselves. She trusts us."

Dr. Jacobs nodded. She had the phone book open and was dialing. "The Beldings live in that condo over on Ryerson Drive," she said. "It's only about ten minutes or so from here if we hurry. Start the car, Ed. We've got to get over there." She glared at the phone. "Damn. It's disconnected or something."

"She must be there already," Shane said hollowly.

"Then we've got to move fast," Dr. Jacobs informed him. "Let's go!"

* * *

Dawn had never been into this area before, even though it was fairly close to her home. The condos had been built in the late eighties; before that the land had been woods. The condo development was very pleasant, with blocks of buildings set back from the parking lots and lawns. It didn't take her long to find the address the phone book had listed for the two teachers.

She walked up the pathway beside the well-tended bushes, her heavy shoulder bag banging against her hip. She had her right hand in the bag, clutching the cold metal revolver she'd taken from her father's drawer. She flicked off the safety catch, and the gun seemed to weigh a ton more in her hand.

She felt sick when she thought about what she had to do. But there was no alternative.

If the Beldings were home, of course. If they weren't —well, she'd figure out something else. She had to, or she and Carolyn were dead.

The door to number 17 was teal blue, the number prominently displayed in brass. It was a ground-floor condo, and she saw that the blinds on the windows were closed. It didn't mean anyone was there, though. They probably had to keep the blinds closed so people couldn't see inside. As she walked up to the door, she heard the sound of a piano inside. She felt a sense of relief that at least one of the teachers was home. Her stomach tightened from nerves.

She had to force herself to ring the doorbell. It took all her courage to stand there and wait. The music stopped, and a moment later the door opened.

It was Mrs. Belding. She was dressed in jeans and a loose T-shirt with her hair caught up in a band. "Yes?"

"Uh, I'm Dawn Jacobs," Dawn said. Her voice was a little squeaky, she was so nervous. "I'm in your husband's literature class. I'm really sorry to bother you on the weekend, but I've *got* to talk to him."

"Oh, sure." The teacher held the door open. "Come on in."

Dawn managed a thin smile and almost stumbled as she stepped inside. There was a short hallway, with several doors leading off from it. On the wall were framed art prints, and there was a coat rack and mirror behind the door. Mrs. Belding closed the door and slipped past Dawn. "This way," she said. Dawn followed her into the living room. There were bookcases, an entertainment unit, and a couch, but the room was dominated by a large white piano, which Mrs. Belding had obviously been playing. Curled up under the piano bench was a large black cat that was dozing. Dawn immediately thought about the familiars that witches were supposed to have.

There was a breakfast nook off to one side and a doorway leading from that to the kitchen. Mr. Belding was seated at the table in the nook, and he glanced up. He had a cup of coffee and a newspaper there and had obviously been reading until she arrived.

"Dawn?" he said, slightly puzzled. "What brings you here? Trouble with the book project?"

"Something like that." Dawn tried to sound casual. The gun felt very heavy, and her palm was sweating slightly. She swallowed, trying to control her nerves.

"You know that place you stayed at for your honeymoon, Balbec? Did you read that book you lent me?"

He smiled. "Sure. Did you like it? I thought it would appeal to you."

"It was—interesting," Dawn answered. "Did you know that they had a plague there four hundred years ago? People going crazy and dying?"

He frowned. "Now you mention it, I do recall something about it. Why?"

"Because people are going crazy here and dying, too." She stared directly at him. She was convinced that he wasn't acting. He honestly didn't know. She glanced at Mrs. Belding, who had returned to sit at the piano. She appeared puzzled, too. Dawn couldn't believe that either of them would have gone along willingly with the parasites. That made what she had to do even harder.

"Yes, it is pretty dreadful," Mr. Belding agreed. "Friends of yours. We heard about Candace, and we're very sorry."

"You must be very upset," Mrs. Belding added sympathetically.

"I'm more than upset," Dawn told them. "I'm infected too. Last night the same parasite that killed Candy, Vince, and Jesse attacked me. Carolyn Rice is also infected."

"Parasite?" Mr. Belding frowned again. "I didn't know that they'd discovered the cause of the disease."

"They haven't," Dawn answered coldly. "But I have. It's the things that you brought back with you from Balbec."

"Things?" Mrs. Belding was genuinely surprised. "What are you talking about? Souvenirs?"

"Parasites," Dawn informed her. "Creatures that live on the mental energies of other people. Things that prey on our dreams. Two of them, one inside each of you."

Mr. Belding stood up. "Dawn," he said gently, "you're obviously very distraught because of your friends. But there's nothing wrong with Toni or me. We're fine."

"No, you're not." Dawn shook her head firmly. "You just don't know about them. But they're there, inside each of you."

Mr. Belding stared at her. "Dawn, listen to me—" He started to move toward her.

Dawn's right hand came out of her bag. Trying not to think about it, she raised the gun, centering it on his chest. Mrs. Belding gasped and Mr. Belding stopped still. "Stay right there," Dawn said. Her voice was flat and emotionless. "If either of you makes a move toward me, I promise, I'll shoot to kill."

CHAPTER

19

Shock, bewilderment, and fear struggled to control the faces of the two teachers. Dawn was scared but determined. She gestured with the gun.

"Over toward the windows," she said, trying to sound forceful and not terrified of what she was doing. *"Move!"*

Mrs. Belding glanced at her husband. He nodded, watching Dawn all the time. Slowly, both of them walked across the room. Dawn wanted to warn them not to make any sudden moves but was afraid it would start to sound like she'd been watching too many bad movies. When the teachers were standing beside the blinds, Dawn said, "Okay, far enough."

"Dawn," Mr. Belding said gently. "You don't know what you're doing. Just put the gun down—"

"No way," Dawn answered coldly. "I *know* exactly what I'm doing. This is self-defense." She kept the gun leveled between the two teachers. "I think you know I mean it when I say that if either of you tries anything, I'll have to shoot."

"Dawn, please," Mrs. Belding said. "Think about what you're doing. This isn't very smart."

"Maybe not," agreed Dawn. "But I'm desperate, and it's all I could think of to save my life and Carolyn's. And to stop any more kids from dying. Now, listen to me. As I said, there are two parasites—cloudy things that prey on mental energy. They're inside each of you, but I believe you don't know it. And they're what has caused this plague of madness and killed my friends. They've infected Carolyn, and last night they got to me. That means I'm going to start hallucinating, being unable to tell dream from reality and it could begin any time. Before it does, I've got to stop those things."

"Are you sure you're able to tell dream from reality right now?" asked Mr. Belding.

"No," agreed Dawn. "Because it's obvious from the previous cases that the victims can't. So maybe I'm hallucinating already." She gestured with the gun. "But *you* can tell the difference, and so can this gun. And if I *am* hallucinating, it won't matter what I do, will it? It'll seem real to me. So listen.

"Those parasites are night creatures. They can't live long in the daylight without hosts. They need people to hide inside. They picked the two of you. Now, in the day, they're most vulnerable. I think it's the only time they can be killed. At night they're too strong, and they can really warp your mind. In the daylight they're weaker. And, while they're inside you two, they're dependent on you for safety and probably other things. I think that if anything happens to either of you, it will kill those creatures. They're tied into you."

Mr. Belding started to move, but Dawn's gesture with the revolver stopped him. "Dawn," he said, fighting to stay calm, "you can't mean what I think you're saying! That's crazy!"

"But I *am* crazy!" Dawn yelled. "They *made* me crazy. And they're going to make me dead—unless I kill them first! So"—she leveled the gun at his chest—"I'm going to have to strike first. To kill them, I'm afraid I'm going to have to kill you." She stared at him coldly. "I'm sorry. I know it's not your fault. But there's no other choice."

Mrs. Belding opened her mouth to scream as Dawn's finger tightened on the trigger. Then—

Two yellowish clouds, like steam, slithered out of the teachers' heads. The wispy, sickly material gathered in the air, writhing and roiling. The scream in Mrs. Belding's throat was cut off as she stared at the disgusting vapors.

"The blinds!" screamed Dawn, relieved and terrified at the same time. "Open the stupid blinds!"

Mr. Belding whirled around and grabbed the blinds. He ripped at them with his hands, not even fumbling for the control rod. The crash as they tore free was almost deafening. A great flood of light filled the room. The two clouds bubbled and slithered in the air, moving away from the window, toward Dawn.

Realizing their intention was to invade her, Dawn gasped and threw herself into a forward roll. Thank goodness for gym class! The clouds passed over her as she hit the carpet, barely missing her. They seemed to be trying desperately to escape from the sunlight. Mrs. Belding opened the other blinds by hand, and the room glowed with light and warmth as the clouds retreated.

"My God," gasped Mr. Belding, shaken. "You were right. Those—those *things* were inside us!"

"Yeah," Dawn agreed, getting shakily to her feet. She still held the gun tightly in her hand. "I'm sorry, but I had to scare them out of you. You had to really believe I was going to kill you. It was the only thing I could think to do to get them to leave you."

The clouds were retreating toward the breakfast nook now, as fast as they could. Parts of their edges seemed to be burning off in the light. Dawn hoped that they were suffering dreadfully.

Then she realized that she'd made a terrible mistake. The clouds weren't running scared. They were moving with a purpose.

Both yellow things suddenly dropped like stones when they were over the piano seat.

The dozing cat gave a yowl of terror and sprang to

its feet as it was enveloped by the two sickly clouds. The parasites shifted and then began to contract, like a net, tightening about their prey. It happened too quickly and unexpectedly for Dawn to react, and in a second the clouds had been absorbed by the wakened and thoroughly terrified cat.

Dawn managed to get into motion at last, raising the gun and aiming. Mrs. Belding grabbed her arm.

"No!" she yelled. "You can't shoot Bandit!"

The gun went off, sending a jarring shock through Dawn's wrist. Because of the teacher's grip, the shot went wild, searing a scar along the side of the piano. The cat leaped straight at Dawn. Tiny teeth sank into her wrist, drawing blood and sending a sharp stab of agony up her arm. Dawn screamed with pain, and the gun fell from her nerveless fingers. The cat, hissing and clawing, turned and ran, spraying blood from Dawn's wrist.

"We've got to stop it!" Dawn yelled, fighting down the pain that was enveloping her arm. "If it gets loose, those parasites could infect someone else! We have to stop it!" Shaking off Mrs. Belding's hand, Dawn dashed after the cat into the kitchen. She was just in time to see the cat flap in the back door slam shut behind the fleeing animal.

If it remained free— Dawn threw open the door and hurtled herself outside and after the cat. There was a flicker of movement in the bushes, and then Bandit shot across the lawn, heading for the open spaces of the parking lot.

Beyond that were woods. If it got into those, there

was no hope of ever finding it. The parasites would find new hosts and wait till Dawn was dead.

She sprinted after the cat as fast as she could. Behind her, she heard the Beldings following. She didn't care whether they intended to help her or stop her. The only thing that was important now was the capture of the cat.

Dawn's heart pounded, and her breath rasped in and out in short gasps as she put on as much speed as she could manage. She knew she was still bleeding from the bite in her wrist, but she forced herself not to think about it. *Die later,* she told herself. *Get the cat now!*

Bandit seemed to be having some kind of fit as it ran, twitching and shaking. The parasites were trying to control its mind, she realized. They were trying to stay alive and clearly couldn't trust the cat to do the right thing instinctively. Perhaps its smaller brain made the cat easier to control than a human host would have been, but Bandit was obviously fighting to regain control. The resulting fight for domination of the cat's body slowed it down.

Dawn was gaining on it.

Everything focused now on the fleeing, twitching animal. She ignored every other sound, every other sight. If she didn't catch the cat, she and Carolyn were dead.

Then the lawn was gone, and there was just asphalt and a few parked cars as Bandit dashed for the woods. Dawn was utterly focused on the creature and oblivious to everything else.

Then something slammed into her from behind, knocking her down and to the side, her legs cut out from under her. Dawn screamed as she crashed onto the hard parking lot surface. Her entire side went numb, then blazed with pain. Gasping, she stared up at Mrs. Belding.

Dawn's first thought was to scratch the teacher's eyes out. *She stopped me!* she thought. *She let her stupid cat get away!* Then she realized what had really happened as her mind refocused.

A car had slid across the lot, brakes squealing furiously, missing her by inches. Dawn had been so intent on the chase that she hadn't even been aware that there was a car heading right for her as she dashed out. Mrs. Belding's tackle had been to stop her and save her life—not the cat's.

Dawn, still prone on the ground, stared at Bandit—or what was left of the poor thing. The car had missed Dawn by inches, but it had slid right into the unfortunate cat. Its mangled, bloody body had been shot across the lot, landing in a heap about twenty feet away. As Dawn stared at it, a pallid yellow mist seeped out of the ruined body. The cloud tried to form, but it was no use. In the bright sunlight, the vapors quickly grew thinner and then vanished altogether.

The parasites were dead.

Dawn almost wished she was. Her left side, where she'd hit the ground, was a mass of pain. Her right wrist, still bleeding, felt almost normal in comparison. And there was a terrible burning sensation in her thigh. She managed a painful smile at Mrs. Belding. "Thank you. You saved my life."

The teacher was too stunned to do anything more than nod and then try to stand up herself. She was bleeding, too, and must have cut herself when she brought Dawn down.

Then there were a whole mess of people around her. Dawn realized that the car that had almost killed her had been her mother's. Talk about irony! Her parents were there, and so was Shane along with both teachers and a handful of other people who must have been around the grounds and had been drawn to the near tragedy. They were all talking at once, and Dawn couldn't make anything out. Her ears were ringing.

Then her mother pushed everyone aside. "I'm a doctor," she snapped. "And that's my daughter." Nobody could argue with that. To the Beldings, she ordered, "Send for an ambulance."

"I'm okay," Dawn managed to say.

"You are not," her mother replied firmly. "You're bleeding all over your skirt and blouse, and you have a bite on your wrist. God knows what other damage."

Dawn laughed. "Oh, that." She lay back, happy she didn't have to get up again, as her mother carefully felt for broken bones. "They're not important. Check my thigh."

"Shane told me you were infected," Mom said. Dawn could see she was in tears.

"They're dead," Dawn answered. "The parasites. Check my leg."

Her mother nodded and lifted the hem of her skirt. Dawn propped herself up on her elbows and looked. As she'd expected, the burning sensation had been the nerve knot. With the death of the parasites it had self-destructed or something. The redness and swelling were gone.

"You're clear," her mother said.

Dawn gave a happy sigh and lay back again. Shane slipped his sweater under her head as a pillow and gave her an encouraging smile. She grinned back. "And I'll bet that Carolyn's has gone, too," she said. "We're clean, all of us. It's over now." She felt a tremendous sense of relief. She didn't even mind the pain too much. She was alive, and Carolyn was safe.

Nobody else in Brookville would die as victims of those horrible creatures. Were there more of them still at large, though? She'd worry about that later. Right now, it was enough to know that the nightmares were over. They were safe to dream again.

Author's Note

For once, some of the books I mention in this story actually do exist. Jacques Vallee's *Passport to Magonia* is a real (and absolutely fascinating) book. If you're at all interested in UFOs, alien encounters, or the legends of fairies and other magical beings, this is a book you should read. You may not agree with everything the author says, but you won't be bored with his arguments!

Charles Fort, too, was a fascinating writer. He collected some very strange stories that make entertaining reading. There's even a Fortean Society, with a newsletter, still in existence. If you're interested in some really strange tales that may (or may not) be true, check out his *The Book of the Damned.* Both Diana Wynne Jones and Esther Friesner are actually authors of fantasy novels that are well worth reading. (Your library can help find any of these books.)

Finally, Ofra Harnoy is also quite real. She's an amazingly talented cellist, and her recordings of Vivaldi are superb. Carolyn is a fan of hers because I am!

About the Author

JOHN PEEL was born in Nottingham, England, the oldest of seven children, and he attended Nottingham University. He moved to the United States to marry his pen pal, Nan. They live in Manorville, New York, with their wire-haired fox terrier, Dashiell, who frequently wants John to stop writing to play ball.

John is the author of numerous science-fiction and mystery novels for young adults, and he has been a contributing editor and writer for several magazines. His novels *Talons, Shattered,* and *Poison* are available from Archway Paperbacks. He has also written *Star Trek: Deep Space Nine®: Prisoners of Peace* for Minstrel Books. John is currently working on two novels for the *Are You Afraid of the Dark?* series, to be published by Minstrel Books this year.